"You still plan to marry a millionaire?"

"Yes, I do," Clarissa said, with more confidence than she felt. She lifted her head high and squared her shoulders.

"Are you a romantic?" Conor asked.

"No!" Clarissa said emphatically, though she backed away flustered. "Not anymore."

"Do you believe in love at first sight?" Conor reached for her hips.

"No!" she said, slapping his hands away.

"Do you believe in listening to your heart?"

"No, it gets me into trouble." She was backed against the refrigerator, with nowhere to go but into his arms. "I will choose a husband who will be able to provide security and stability for my son and me. A millionaire would do nicely."

"Then kiss me," Conor challenged with deadly calm.

Dear Reader,

Picture this: You're thirty, single and on a husband hunt! You've done your research, highlighted the eligible bachelors, made lists and spreadsheets, bar graphs and flow charts...and you've narrowed your choices to a millionaire, a cowboy and the boy next door.

That's exactly what three American Romance heroines have done—and we're about to pick up their stories in the hilarious HOW TO MARRY... trilogy. In *A Million-Dollar Man* you'll meet the first bride-in-waiting, but don't forget to watch for *One Hot Cowboy* by Cathy Gillen Thacker and *The Bad Boy Next Door* by Mindy Neff.

Find out if these three men can show these three women a thing or two about passion—the most important part of a marriage!

Happy reading!

Debra Matteucci
Senior Editor & Editorial Coordinator
Harlequin Books
300 East 42nd Street
New York, NY 10017

HOW TO MARRY...

A MILLION-DOLLAR MAN

Vivian Leiber

Harlequin Books

TORONTO • NEW YORK • LONDON
AMSTERDAM • PARIS • SYDNEY • HAMBURG
STOCKHOLM • ATHENS • TOKYO • MILAN
MADRID • WARSAW • BUDAPEST • AUCKLAND

ISBN 0-373-16672-9

A MILLION-DOLLAR MAN

Copyright © 1997 by Arlynn Leiber Presser.

Printed in U.S.A.

Prologue

The last plaintive wails of Meat Loaf's "Two Out of Three Ain't Bad" was winding down on the jukebox when Conor and Bill finished their burgers.

"Come on, stay for a while, Conor, we'll have fun," Bill urged.

Conor pulled a few bills from his wallet to pay the check. He shook his head. "I gotta work."

"You always gotta work. We're still kids, Conor. We just got out of school. This summer we're supposed to be enjoying our last fling. You know—" he nudged his buddy "—party hardy!"

Bill would have pressed the point. Then he remembered. He could enjoy this final summer of childhood, because his future was already certain. In September, his father would get him his union card and he'd be guaranteed his job as a plumber.

But Conor wasn't so lucky.

Bill knew that Conor's dad, never one with a steady job in the first place, had left two months ago. Bill didn't say anything, figuring since Conor didn't confide in him, he wasn't even supposed to know. Bill's mom had only found out because she was a relentless gossip.

Since his dad left, Conor had scrounged a half-dozen jobs as a handyman for small projects no one else wanted to handle. He was good with his hands, had a reputation for meticulous work and he finished every job he started. On time and on budget. He even had business backed up.

Bill wondered how Conor would get his union card, but figured he'd better not ask.

Conor finished the last of his soda, put it on the counter, then turned his head to look out the window at the SummerFest roller boller and target shoot booths. There were pony rides, a merry-go-round, too, even a roller coaster that plunged at the end of Webster Street and snaked along Roosevelt Avenue and back again.

It didn't look the same to him. Not the same as last summer when he hadn't a care in the world. That roller coaster had been a SummerFest favorite to him and Bill—up and down until they both felt sick. Happy but sick.

He was a man now, a seventeen-year-old man with a mom and two sisters to support. A rent bill overdue. The utility companies threatening to cut off service. Even working as hard as he did, he couldn't keep up.

He continued to grimly stare out the window. Then, as the crowd ebbed and flowed around three girls who hesitated at the fortune-teller's tent, he saw her.

His heart jumped, his eyes widened. He pulled the red-and-white checked curtains of Jimmy's Diner apart to get a better look.

Tendrils of wavy flame red hair escaped from the single braid that hung halfway down her back. Someone's attempt to tame the wild mass had been in vain. Her faded plaid dress, mended at its collar, was way too small—its hem came up high on legs that were coltish and bruised.

Conor felt more than just the usual reflexive, nearly embarrassing stirrings at the thought of anything female.

She was with two other girls. Conor figured the trio for early teens. But the redhead was the one who caught his attention, something about her spoke to him in a way that he hadn't heard before from any of the girls in his neighborhood.

She didn't even look toward the hamburger shack that he and Bill thought of as a second home. Yet, the way she held her shoulders made him think she was like him, someone who had met with bad fortune and who was determined to overcome every obstacle. She was a fighter, he was sure of it, but not so hard-edged that she couldn't see the beauty in life. She'd grow into a proud but sensitive woman.

Bill stood, pushing his wire rim glasses up his nose and worrying the tiny bald spot that was already developing on the back of his head.

"Whatcha doin'? Looking at little kids?" he accused.

"'Course not. But who is she?"

"The redhead? I don't know her name—Claire, or something—but I know she hasn't got no family around here. Least, not any family that wants her."

"How'd that happen?"

"You'd have to ask my mom," Bill said, leaning on the windowsill to get a better look at the girls who had paused in front of the gaudy fortune-teller's tent. "Apparently, she gets passed around a little every year. For the last three months, she's been taking care of some old geezer who was a second cousin to one of her dead folks. When he dies, who knows who'll take her?" Bill paused before saying anything further. "The blonde I think is from Parkdale two blocks over and the other one, from what I hear, is her cousin from Texas. She's a down-home dish, don't you think? Betcha she's gonna be a model."

"How old is she? The redhead, I mean," Conor asked, staring at her, transfixed, watching her giggle with her friends as the blonde handed her camera to a passerby so that all three girls could be included in a photo in front of the tent.

The redhead pulled at the hem of her dress. He liked her smile, even if her amber eyes never quite lost their haunted look.

"Why do you want to know all this? Are you going to talk to her?" Bill asked, with a screwed-up look on his face.

Conor turned to stare at his longtime friend before asking the girl's age for a second time.

"She's twelve, Conor. She's in sixth grade at Parker Public. You're seventeen years old. You're losing it, my friend."

Conor glanced in her direction before shrugging at his friend.

"I don't want to talk to her. Too young."

"Good. Forget about her. Besides, she's one of

those nice girls. Goes to church every Sunday even though the old man couldn't care less what she does. Not your type.''

They shared a smile. Conor could tell that Bill, too, was thinking about the girls who chased after Conor. Girls couldn't get enough of his dark, wavy hair, his baby blues, and his smooth, tight muscles.

Blondes, Conor liked them blond. And a little wild. Easy to talk to. Easy to take. Just plain easy.

When Bill was lucky, sometimes the girls would find out they liked him just as much. But Conor was always the one they noticed first.

"Forget about her," Bill said, pulling Conor from the window.

Conor did forget her, caught up so quickly in the concerns of work and raising two sisters. But some part of his mind would, he was sure, hold on to the memory long after this SummerFest was over.

THOUGH IT WAS LATE August, Clarissa shivered, pulling the worn plaid cotton over her knees. Sabrina was, on every other day of the year, simply the lady who lived in the apartment over the newsstand. But on SummerFest weekend, she was a mysterious seer with burning incense, a crystal ball, and a firm fix on the future. The tent wasn't just a piece of canvas thrown over a plywood frame—it was the vortex of fate and destiny. Little Maurice wasn't simply a friendly monkey—he was a familiar with eerie, nearly human features. Clarissa leaned forward to hear Sabrina intone over her friend Hallie's palm.

"You're going to marry the boy next door," Sabrina said, crouching low over Hallie's outstretched fingers.

"Somebody else better move into Parkdale," Maggie teased as Hallie blushed. "There's no way your mom's going to let you marry Cody Brock."

"When you get married, you don't have to have your parents' permission," Hallie said primly.

"You have a crush on him!" Maggie accused.

"Wouldn't be surprising," Clarissa said with a nod. "All the girls at school do. He's really cute. But he gets into so much trouble."

"Do you want to marry him?" Maggie leaned forward to interrogate her cousin.

Hallie shrugged with forced nonchalance. "I just want my fortune read, all right?"

Maggie and Clarissa shared a conspiratorial smile as Sabrina continued to map out Hallie's fate. But even while they giggled over each new revelation, Clarissa felt a tightening in her throat, a little worry.

She knew it was silly to think Sabrina had special powers, but she was scared that Sabrina would discover a new fortune in her hand, a different fate than the one she had predicted last summer. One Clarissa liked just fine. Maybe she would see something not so wonderful. Maybe she'd see a future that everyone in Bridgeport could have guessed was waiting for Clarissa—no home, no family, no security.

"My turn next," Maggie insisted, as Hallie got up from the three-legged stool in front of Sabrina. She flipped her hair from her face in a gesture at once so casual and yet so studied. Clarissa wished she had

Maggie's beauty, though Maggie was so nice that the wish never turned to envy.

"I see a ranch," Sabrina said, squinting at Maggie's palm. "And a cowboy."

"You'll marry a cowboy!" Hallie exclaimed, clapping her hands.

Sabrina wagged a gnarled finger in Maggie's face.

"But he won't be on your list," she said sternly.

"I like the cowboy part," Maggie said. "But I don't understand the part about a list. What does that mean?"

Sabrina shook her head.

"I only read the palms. I don't interpret them."

"Maybe Sabrina's saying you'll have a list of men to choose from," Hallie suggested. "So you can line them up and pick the handsomest. Kind of like one of those livestock auctions you took me to last summer."

Given Maggie's beauty, the notion of a lineup of attractive men vying for her hand was not outrageous to Clarissa—just funny in a naughty sort of way. She laughed, but as her friends dissolved into shrieks of mirth, her throat felt tight and her voice muted.

She was worried. Even though she knew it was dumb to put any stock in a fortune-teller's words.

As the two girls regained their seriousness, Sabrina motioned to Clarissa to sit for her palm reading. Clarissa swallowed hard. She crossed her fingers in the frayed pocket of her dress.

She sat and slowly held out her pale, freckled hand.

Sabrina smiled kindly and Clarissa remembered that, beneath the jeweled turban, lived a neighbor. Clarissa had even taken care of Maurice for several days the previous month when Sabrina had to go out of town to visit her daughter.

"Clarissa, please don't worry," Sabrina said. "I still see that millionaire of yours."

Clarissa let go of a breath she hadn't even known she had been holding.

"You'll have two children and you will travel," Sabrina continued gently. "And you will be a very happy woman with love and laughter to follow all of your days."

Twirling a stray curl of her hair on her finger, Clarissa's emotions soared from longing to outright excitement.

"Will I have a mansion?"

"You asked her that last year," Maggie said good-naturedly. "Tell her, Sabrina. Tell her all about the mansion. Don't leave anything out."

"I see a big house, very big. Many, many rooms. And a lot of happiness in each."

"Wow," Clarissa said, staring at her palm. "Very big?"

"The biggest," Sabrina reassured her. "It will be very close to here."

"How can a millionaire live in Bridgeport?" Hallie asked, skeptical. "A millionaire should live in the Gold Coast neighborhood."

"When she says very near, it could be anywhere," Maggie said, with a wink and a reassuring smile. "It's just like the 'list' she says I'm going to choose my husband from. Who knows what it means?"

"There is a very special millionaire for Clarissa who will live near here," Sabrina said to the girls.

"But Clarissa will have to find him. She will have to seek him out."

"Will he be handsome?" Clarissa asked.

"So handsome that you will be unable to resist him."

Maggie fell backward on her stool in an exaggerated swoon. "Oh, darling, darling, I can't resist you...or your millions!" she mugged.

Hallie giggled.

Sabrina commanded them both to silence with a narrowing of her kohl-rimmed eyes. As the two girls sobered, she peered into Clarissa's palm once more.

"He is there," she whispered, sensing Clarissa's fears and worries. "Be patient for he won't make his appearance immediately. But remember! You will have to discover him yourself."

Clarissa brought her palm up to her face as if she were studying a priceless gem. She caressed the lines Sabrina had pointed out to her.

A handsome husband.

Wealthy, too.

Children and a home to call her own.

Nothing could make her feel more wonderful than the few minutes that the girls spent in this tent.

The future mapped out by Sabrina was a complete contrast to the life Clarissa knew. She was tall and gawky, and her hand-me-down clothes only seemed to accentuate her thin legs. The boys called her "giraffe." And she didn't have a home, much less a mansion. Closest thing she had was a cheap suitcase that had once belonged to her mother. And she had used the suitcase often enough. One strap was broken and the lining smelled.

She held the precious future to her breast and closed her eyes for just one more moment of dreaming. The dream would have to last her for a while, at least until next summer when Sabrina would once again don her turban and proclaim herself a gypsy seer.

NEARLY TWENTY YEARS LATER, Clarissa Mc-Shaunessy was thirty years old, homeless and flat broke. She had a seven-year-old boy. No husband.

And there weren't any millionaires in sight.

Chapter One

Sabrina stood at the paisley scarf door of her tent, watching the final twilight hours of the SummerFest in Chicago's Bridgeport neighborhood. The carnies were taking down the prizes from the game boards and those at the roller coaster and the merry-go-round were telling the people in line that theirs would be the last ride. The horses were eating their apple treats. Vendors hosed the sticky cotton candy machine. The roller boller hawker waved at her. She acknowledged him with a slight, nearly imperious nod.

She was waiting for Clarissa. She had heard the rumors, that Clarissa's eight-year-old marriage had ended abruptly. That Clarissa had come back to Bridgeport, still searching for that elusive sense of love and home that she never had as a girl. Sabrina figured Clarissa would be drawn to the fortune-telling tent. After all, Sabrina had always tried to tell her good news, good news the girl had so desperately needed to hear.

Toddlers' heads drooped on their fathers' shoulders, couples made plans for dinner in nearby restaurants.

The band played a final limp polka. Sabrina started to wonder if perhaps Clarissa wouldn't come.

The carnival was nearly over.

Everyone had seen enough, eaten enough, ridden enough and played enough for the annual weekend carnival. And Sabrina had read so many palms, assuaging worries and giving hope—every other day of the year, her words would be regarded as the meddling of an old woman.

For SummerFest, she was Madame Sabrina—to be listened to with mouth agape and heart aflutter.

Sabrina started to back into the tent, but stopped. She noticed from the corner of her eye a stirring in the crowd.

Heads turned as a redhead strode through the arcade aisles, carrying a bulging leather backpack, hand firmly grasped by a solemn little boy whose hair was more like carrots than his mother's flame locks.

She was beautiful, as Sabrina had always known she would grow up to be. Tall and lanky in inch-heeled cowboy boots, hips tugging her faded blue jeans at each step. Her hair hung halfway down on her back in full, rich curls. Her amber eyes, rimmed with jet lashes, searched the game tents but never acknowledged the men who appraised her.

She was out for fun, desperate even, but not for the kind they had in mind.

"Hey, Red!" A carnie called from behind the duck target booth. He shrugged when she didn't turn around, as if to say "some women don't know what they're missing."

Sabrina smiled and tugged at her turban to make sure it was in place.

She had one more fortune to tell this evening.

"MOM, IT'S OUR LAST dollar," Tommy said, a worried expression on his face. "We can't use it at a carnival."

Clarissa defiantly tilted up her chin and wiped a speck of dust from her eye. She wouldn't allow herself tears. Not in front of her son.

"Tommy, if you only have one dollar left to your name, you have to use it for something fun. It's bad luck to do anything else."

"But what will we do tomorrow? When we're broke? When we don't have any place to stay?"

Clarissa took a deep breath and looked at her boy. "Tomorrow is...tomorrow." She sighed, wishing she had something so much wiser to say. "It's a long ways away. You're too young to worry so much. Let me do the worrying for both of us. Tonight, let's have fun. Just one night. Then we can go back to...to worrying."

"I don't want to go back."

"I don't either, Tommy. I don't either."

She switched her backpack from one shoulder to another and continued on her way, stopping once to point out the Ferris wheel to Tommy. He just shook his head, his mouth downturned. He didn't seem to care that there was fun to be had.

They walked through the kiddie land games and the booths where the goldfish were sold and faces painted for a dollar. She pointed out each booth, encouraged him, pushed him. But he was adamant. Nothing looked good to him.

Then they turned the corner to what they hadn't known they were looking for: Madame Sabrina's Fortunes.

Maybe in some part of her mind, she was looking for it and yet, when she stood right in front of that tent, she was startled that it was there. The gaudy paisley fabric covering the khaki tent had faded, the sign proclaiming Sabrina's powers had lost its sheen, the outrageous promises of accuracy about the future had all but disappeared.

Clarissa's eyes at once widened, her lips parted, and then, as if remembering some memory once beautiful, once fun, and now tarnished, her shoulders drooped with defeat.

But then the curtain parted and a single bejewelled and wrinkled hand emerged.

"Dollar for your fortune," a heavily accented voice enticed.

"It was only a quarter the last time I was here," Clarissa protested. "And, besides, you're terrible at telling the future."

Dark, kohl-lined eyes peered from the folds of the tent, studying Clarissa and her boy.

"No, Clarissa, you just haven't made your future yet."

Tommy tugged at his mother's elbow. "Mom, here's where I want to spend the dollar," he said.

"But, Tommy, I thought you didn't want to spend our last buck," Clarissa said, suddenly feeling the shiver of cold, so familiar, that she had felt every time she had entered Sabrina's tent.

What if Sabrina didn't see a wonderful fortune?

"Let's spend our last dollar on tomorrow," he said, shaking his head and pointing to Sabrina.

"I TOLD YOU that you were going to marry a millionaire," Sabrina said archly, raising a provocative eyebrow as she studied Clarissa. "And you will."

The paisley scarves covering the khaki tent canvas looked worn. The patchouli incense made her nose tickle. The crystal ball on the table in front of Sabrina looked as if it had a crack running through it that Clarissa didn't remember from her childhood. And Sabrina herself looked a little less sure of herself. Maybe it was the spandex tights which she wore, instead of the lace-and-sequined peasant skirt Clarissa recalled.

Sabrina's bracelets jangled defiantly. She glanced once at the boy, who was soberly scratching her pet monkey's fur. The monkey responded with a high-pitched purr of pleasure.

"You told me I'd marry a millionaire," Clarissa said. She leaned forward to whisper quietly in Sabrina's ear. "And I ended up marrying a no-account who drank too much and took up with a younger woman. He left me for a dancer, and I'm not talking ballerina."

Sabrina snorted. "I didn't say what would happen in between growing up and marrying your millionaire. And I always told you that you had to find him, not the other way around."

"Oh, Sabrina, this is ridiculous. What am I doing talking to you when I should be out there..."

"Out there doing what?"

"Making my future."

Clarissa was tired. At thirty she had nothing more to her name than a failed marriage, a worn pair of jeans, thousands of dollars in credit card debt made by her husband and a half-carat engagement ring that she knew she would have to sell.

She also had a seven-year-old son who needed her, depended on her.

She couldn't fail him.

And the fact that she didn't have anything to give him broke her heart.

If she had asked him, he would have told her she was a wonderful mommy, that she loved him and that was the most important thing. But she wasn't willing to ask him whether she had failed him. Those kind of questions hurt too much to ask. She only wanted to do better, to give him better than she had had herself.

"It's been a long time since you've come back to Bridgeport," Sabrina observed.

"True. It's been eight years," Clarissa said. "But I thought I'd find a home. I just traded one suitcase for another. We moved so many times, following my husband, that I sometimes didn't have time to unpack. But now that I've come back to Bridgeport I know the terrible truth. There's nothing here for me now. All the McShaunessys are either dead or gone."

She wondered what impulse had made her confide her troubles in Sabrina. Clarissa was ordinarily a very private person. She hadn't even told Maggie or Hallie that her marriage was over—and she was sure that both would find it shocking. She had never told them anything but good news.

"I don't know where to go next," she said.

"Home is where you make it," Sabrina murmured.

"I don't have too much to make it with."

"Are you saying you're giving up?"

Clarissa looked at her son.

"Never," she said vehemently.

"Then let me look at your future again," Sabrina said, her voice low and throaty, seductive in its own way, enticing Clarissa to surrender her palm. "Just one more time, Clarissa. Let me take one look."

Clarissa hesitated and then, lulled by the voice of her best youthful memories, held her hand out to the seer.

Was she being silly to listen to Sabrina? Sabrina was no oracle, Clarissa told herself. She was just a woman who made a little extra cash by working at a neighborhood carnival.

While Sabrina studied her hand, Clarissa caught Tommy's eye.

She would do anything for her son.

She was strong.

She was determined.

She would get a home for him.

"You're still going to marry that millionaire," Sabrina mused, peering at the lines on Clarissa's hand. "You want it very badly, and you'll have it. A home of your own, a wealthy husband who will adore you and your boy, the security..."

"It's a fantasy," Clarissa said abruptly, snatching her hand from the seer.

Sabrina grabbed her wrist.

"You want it! All of it!" she cried. "If only for him, you want it! So why not go after it? Why not find your millionaire?"

Tommy came to stand beside his mom, touching her shoulder protectively. Clarissa almost stood to leave, but something hypnotic about Sabrina's jet-colored eyes kept her rooted to the dusty floor.

"How do you know so much about me?" Clarissa asked softly. "I haven't come back here to have my fortune read in at least twelve years. How do you even remember me?"

"You make an impression on every person you meet, Clarissa," Sabrina said. "And besides, it's here, in your palm. Mother and father died young. You went from home to home. You struggled to pay your way through college. You've had a very, very hard life...."

She glanced at Tommy and let her sentence trail off into silence. Still, her arthritic finger traced a line along Clarissa's soft, pale flesh.

"You were there when one of your aunts fell ill," Sabrina continued. "You nursed her until her dying day. You cared for another elderly relative and then you married, giving as much to your husband as you did to others you love. But it didn't work out, did it?"

Clarissa swallowed the dry, pungent air. She looked at her son.

"No, it didn't," Tommy said, unsmiling.

"But, here, look at this line," Sabrina said, pointing to a spot on Clarissa's palm. "*He* is there."

Clarissa looked but didn't see anything.

"What do you mean?" Tommy asked, peering over

his mother's shoulder to study her hand. "Who is there?"

"He is. Your mother's millionaire. See where the line splits into two different strands?"

"Kind of," Clarissa said.

"It's right there, Mom. I can see it. I can definitely see it."

"Wishful thinking," Clarissa muttered.

"Your millionaire is there," Sabrina said, nodding approvingly at the boy. "With a house, more children, security. Right there, if your life follows this path. Oh, and he's handsome, sexy, a rogue, a little risqué. But, still, very much a gentleman."

"What about where her fortune forks in the other direction?" Tommy asked, pointing to his mother's palm as if he were studying a map.

"There?" Sabrina's eyes darted to Tommy and then she shrugged and muttered a quick prayer. "There is disaster. Very bad. Don't want to follow that path in life."

Clarissa pulled her hand away and stared at the palm.

"If you're so certain I'm going to marry a millionaire, then why do I have this fork in the road? I mean, in my palm?"

"Because your life could go in two directions right now. You're thirty, right?"

Clarissa nodded.

"Thirty is the most important birthday for a woman. It is a moment when the stars and the fates collide," Sabrina said. "What happens before is out of your hands, but after the stars cross the meridian of thirty, it is choices you make now that create the tenor of life to follow."

"How do you know I'll choose correctly?"

"Because no matter what, Clarissa, I know that you never give up, you have more gumption and courage than any woman on earth, and besides, you're going to look very beautiful in diamonds."

"This is ridiculous! I'm getting us out of here right now!" Clarissa exclaimed, grabbing Tommy's hand.

But he dug his heels into the dirt and brought her up short.

"Mom, she might be right!"

"That I should marry a millionaire?"

"Yeah," Tommy said defiantly. "If you're going to marry, if I'm going to have a daddy, wouldn't somebody with money and a job be better than someone who doesn't have either one?"

Clarissa crouched to be eye to eye with her son.

"Tommy, it's not a millionaire that I want. I just want you to feel secure and happy, to give you all the chances I never had, to make sure you have all the love in the world. The things every child deserves."

"Clarissa, you've always been a strong girl," Sabrina observed. "You've become the kind of woman who can reach for the stars. Remember the dreams you had as a girl—you wanted a millionaire, a gracious and elegant home, a family to call your own. Clarissa, you were made for better than this."

Clarissa sighed, thinking all the dreams of her childhood were so...out of reach.

"Mom," Tommy said, brushing an errant curl from her forehead. "Mom, I already do have all the love in the world. You've given me that. But, Mom, since even before Dad left us, things have gone from bad to worse. You've tried, but look at us. We're not doing too good, are we?"

"No," Clarissa said, tears welling in her eyes. She brushed away the too long bangs from Tommy's forehead. "I guess we're not. But I'm going to change that."

"I always knew you would," Sabrina whispered, slipping the dollar bill Clarissa had given her into Tommy's back pants pocket.

A COUPLE WEEKS later a new, very sophisticated Clarissa McShaunessy stood at the arched doorway of Cathedral Hall, the ninth floor dining room of the University Club—a private club where the cream of Chicago society met. She straightened her back, trying for a regal posture. Her eyes raked the crowd gathering for cocktails, looking for one special man.

She licked her lips one more time, her only concession to nerves. She hoped she wouldn't ruin her makeup. She wasn't used to wearing so much.

She was crashing.

Again.

This time a dinner for Fred Tannenbaum, president and CEO of Tannenbaum Industries. According to the *Chicago Tribune* Clarissa had read yesterday morning, Fred Tannenbaum had come to Chicago for a month to close a deal on supplying oil to a Midwest distributor.

Clarissa was ready for him.

She had done her homework, spending her lunch

hour at the Harold Washington Public Library photo-copying everything she could find on the wealthy wid-ower. Putting all of it into a file folder and taking the bus back to her part-time job substitute teaching at the posh Latin School.

Fred Tannenbaum, according to the press clippings, was a forty-five-year-old widower who had never lived outside of Oklahoma. His net worth was estimated by the major business magazines at fifty million dollars in American-held assets alone.

The gossip columns linked him with stars, society women, heiresses and a couple of foreign princesses—but not all at the same time.

He was everything Clarissa could want in a man: stability, and an apparent absence of vices. And lots and lots and lots of money.

She had pulled out the file and read everything while the hairdresser Pablo Cassini pulled her hair into a sleek French twist. She asked Pablo yet again if he would do something to tone down the flamelike hue of her hair.

"Wouldn't it look a little more…upper-class if I were a blonde or brunette or at least a little more subtle auburn?" Clarissa suggested.

"Oh, no, no!" Pablo protested with Gallic indig-nation. "Your hair is so beautiful I wouldn't dream of touching it with color. *Mais non,* I will not allow even a tint."

After Pablo finished his work, a makeup artist pow-dered her nose just a little, at Clarissa's insistence, to cover the sprinkling of freckles across her nose. Then the artist used a quick swipe of mascara, since Clarissa's lashes were naturally lush and dark.

After a pedicure and manicure, Clarissa slipped into the red evening gown she had hung in the salon's cloakroom. It pulled her shoulders and plunged down her back, hugged every curve of her breasts and puddled at the floor. A slit high up the side revealed Clarissa's long leg.

"Mon Dieu," Pablo murmured. "I never knew a redhead who could wear that color!"

He scrambled in his makeup kit and produced the perfect complementary shade of fire-engine red lipstick.

"You're going to stop traffic," he said, shaking his head like a proud mother.

But Clarissa didn't care about traffic. She was trying to remember every fact she had learned in the last hour about an Oklahoma oilman whose party she would attend.

"Thanks, Pablo," she said, as she pulled several carefully folded hundred dollars from her red evening bag. She took a deep breath as she put the bills into Pablo's hand. She'd hocked her engagement ring at a discreet little pawn shop around the corner. "Can I leave my backpack here and pick it up tomorrow?"

"Of course," Pablo said with a smirk. Clarissa knew he wondered about his eccentric new client who always paid in cash, who seemed to own nothing but ravishing evening gowns and a single pair of jeans and cowboy boots. But she couldn't confide in the man. If she did, every gossip in the city would know her story.

On the way over to the University Club, it was as

Pablo had predicted. Men and women both turned their heads, wondering if they had seen Clarissa on the cover of a magazine or in a recent movie. One cab rammed the back of another on Oak Street as the driver craned his neck for a peek at her legs. And the traffic cop at Michigan and Huron forgot to stop blowing his whistle as he watched her pass. Fortunately, no one was hurt.

She was dressed to impress, though she was only concerned about impressing Fred Tannenbaum, who had no idea what was in store for him that evening.

Clarissa felt as though she were dressed for battle.

And now, at the doorway of the University Club's Cathedral Hall dining room, she was ready for the first skirmish. Getting into the party in Fred's honor without an invitation.

On the other hand, she'd been crashing parties for a month since Sabrina had sent her on her way with a few kisses for good luck. And a stern, nearly frantic, warning to stay away from poverty-stricken males.

Private gallery openings, corporate-sponsored charity balls, receptions for the consulates, the yacht races. Anything and everything where the wealthy converged, Clarissa had showed up. With a little brash confidence, some gently worn designer originals, and a good dose of determination.

Along the way, she had learned that a beautiful woman dressed as if she belonged, head tilted as if she truly were at ease—that kind of woman would seldom be questioned. And never turned away.

She stood at the entrance to the Cathedral Hall, lifted her chin just a little, and smoothed the tight silk knit of her dress. The maître d', whom she had spoken to once before at the club's party to celebrate the opening of the opera season, strode up to meet her. But as he approached, an older man grabbed his arm to greet him.

Clarissa started to bite her nails and then remembered that she had just spent good money getting them done. She wondered if she could sneak downstairs to the telephone booth and call to check on Tommy, who was being baby-sat by a Latin School ninth grader.

"Don't you just hate these things?" A man's voice said.

Clarissa turned and looked into the deepest, bluest eyes she had ever seen. Those eyes were the only boyish quality about this man, tall and rugged, with a sharp jaw and a nose that had the telltale slant of a fighter. Clarissa took in the denim shirt, the tight jeans, the black cowboy boots.

Danger! A voice inside her head reminded. And she remembered Sabrina's warnings. And remembered that fork in the road on her palm.

She looked down at her palms before squeezing them shut and gazed into the club dining room, glittering as it was with sequined gowns and sparkling candlelight. Clarissa's heart was in overdrive, but the rest of her was definitely on red alert.

"I hardly know what you mean," Clarissa sniffed.

"I'm sorry. I should have introduced myself. Conor James."

The name meant nothing to her. She ignored his outstretched hand.

"How 'bout you and me slip out for a hamburger?"

he asked, ignoring her snub and coming behind her so that his breath touched her naked shoulders. The hairs on the back of her neck stood. "Wouldn't a burger with onions, lettuce, tomato and a side order of fries be a lot more fun than the caviar and sun-dried tomato canapés they've got here?"

Actually, it would, Clarissa thought. One of the terrible things about crashing every upper-class party in sight was that the dainty food served was never filling and, besides, she hardly ever knew what she was eating.

A hamburger, now that sounded great! She hadn't treated herself to much of anything, since she had to save every dime for Cassini's salon and the second-hand designer dress shop down the street from her swanky new Gold Coast apartment.

She licked her lips.

"Mmm, I like it when you do that," he murmured.

Clarissa squeezed her hands tightly, almost feeling the crease of the two futures Sabrina had laid out for her.

"Sorry, I'm busy," she said curtly. She gathered the fabric of her dress and sauntered to the maître d' without a backward glance.

It had taken every ounce of her self-discipline to walk away from the intriguing stranger. But she was on a mission. And she wasn't going to be sidetracked by her lousy judgment in men.

She was out to marry a millionaire and there was one very eligible one who was here tonight—Fred Tannenbaum.

"Hello, Nick," she said to the maître d'. Though

her knees were shaking, she hoped her smile was open and warm. She genuinely liked the debonair master of the room.

If Nick was going to throw her out, he reconsidered. Instead, he nodded a solicitous greeting.

"Good evening, Miss...uh..."

"McShaunessy."

"Of course. Miss McShaunessy, how wonderful to see you again, and have a wonderful evening," he said, hesitating before he headed for the entranceway to greet more guests.

Clarissa looked over the maître d's shoulder at the sexy man who had spoken to her. He slouched against the doorjamb, hands in his jeans pockets, his stare rakish, his smile a sexual sneer.

He could be a busboy, or maybe a friend of one of the people who worked in the kitchen, or maybe one of the workmen hired for the remodeling work on the twelfth floor gallery.

But, whoever he was, he didn't belong.

And she had no business looking at him.

Not even for a minute.

He was just the sort of man she'd be attracted to— but not tonight, not when she was mapping out her and her son's future.

She shivered at the memory of his breath upon her skin, then turned away abruptly, accepting a glass of champagne from the tray of a passing waiter.

She scanned the room, looking for the face, the man—Fred Tannenbaum—and mentally reviewed everything she had memorized from the file she had amassed that afternoon.

Chapter Two

"Tsk, tsk, tsk. Mr. James, you must remember the rules," Nick chided, wagging his finger at Conor.

"I remember the rules all right, but I don't live by them," Conor replied amiably, watching the tightly packed crowd until he could no longer pick out the redhead.

Something about her seemed achingly familiar, yet he was sure that if he had seen her before he would have remembered. If only because she was so snooty. He hated the type.

"Can I get you a suit jacket and a tie?" Nick suggested. "We always keep one in back for men who forget...and for those who are determined to flaunt their lower-class origins."

From anyone else, that last comment would have provoked a quick clip at the jaw. Or at the very least an icy stare. But from Nick, it was part of the usual easy banter the two men often exchanged. It was impossible to take offense at Nick.

"Nick, I'm sure you have great jackets back there. But none I'd want to wear. Thanks."

"I'm sure something I've got will fit your shoulders," Nick persisted. "Might be a little tight."

"No, no, no, I don't want to dress up in a monkey suit," Conor said, shaking his head. "I've just come by to say hello to Fred Tannenbaum. We did a few deals way back when. I heard he was in town and that his new partners were giving him a reception."

"You're on the guest list." Nick was known for his photographic memory of guest lists, arcane etiquette and family trees.

"My secretary told me something like that."

"But you won't wear a jacket?"

Conor shook his head.

"Mr. Tannenbaum is still downstairs in the meeting room," Nick advised.

"Then I'll say hello there and won't bother with the party," Conor said, and turned toward the oak-banistered staircase. He paused. "Oh, Nick."

"Yes, sir?"

"Who's the redhead?"

"Oh," Nick murmured with a hint of what sounded to be suppressed pleasure. "That's Miss McShaunessy."

"New around here?"

"Yes, but I'm not sure what family she's from. And frankly," he said, leaning forward confidentially. "I don't recall her name on the guest list."

"She's crashing?" Conor asked. For some reason the idea gave him pleasure.

The two men looked back into the crowd, their eyes settling on the beautiful Miss McShaunessy, who

looked perfectly at home chatting with the head of
Chicago's biggest commodities house.

"I wouldn't throw her out, would you?" Conor
asked.

"No, I wouldn't," Nick confessed. "Besides, if she
turned out to be somebody's sister and I threw her out,
I could be out of a job."

"Must be the McShaunessys of Baltimore."

"Of course," Nick said, brightening. "An old Baltimore family. Rich as all get-out. Shopping centers is
where they made their money. She must be one of the
nieces."

"So she's old money," Conor said derisively.

Nick tactfully ignored his slur.

Conor was sure he had crossed paths with her some-
time deep in his past—though he could remember
nothing of the Baltimore McShaunessys except for a
crotchety old man he had built a mall for. And Conor
had always favored blondes. Had dated only a few
select dark-haired beauties.

But redheads?

Redheaded heiresses?

None that he could remember.

AFTER CAREFULLY wrapping her evening gown into
the dry cleaner's plastic bag and hanging it carefully
in the closet, Clarissa put on a comfortable oversize
T-shirt and snuggled into the sleeping bag at the foot
of Tommy's bed.

"Sure you don't want the bed, Mom?" he asked,
looking up from his comic book. "You look pretty
beat."

"No, I'm fine. It's like camping out."

"Then let me do it. I like camping."

"No, you just read and go to sleep. Tomorrow's a school day."

"Mom, it's only nine o'clock. And I don't need the bed. Remember, when we both had to sleep in sleeping bags at that shelter? I slept fine. You were the one who could never get any rest."

Each word her son spoke was like a knife stabbing into her heart. Seven-year-olds shouldn't know about dads who don't pay rent, shouldn't know about being broke, shouldn't know about hunger and panic and cold and sleeping in homeless shelters. *Well, at least now I've got a plan,* she thought.

"You sleep in the bed," she said resolutely.

"I call dibs on the sleeping bag this weekend," Tommy bargained.

"All right, but go back to reading. I've got lesson plans to review. A teacher, especially a substitute, should never enter a room full of wild second graders without a strategy."

She laid out her lesson plans on the tiger maple parquet floor. *This would be a fantastic place to live if we could afford furniture,* she thought.

The address was impeccable, on one of the poshest streets in the Gold Coast neighborhood of Chicago, a building that reeked money, class, old-world charm. Certainly nothing Clarissa could ever afford if it was at market price, but she knew appearances were everything. This evening had confirmed her notion.

When Tannenbaum had dropped her off in his

rented limousine, he noticed the address, commenting on the architecture in a studiously casual way.

Clarissa was sure that the address alone made Fred aware that she was not merely a potential plaything. She was definitely not mistress material. No, she was wife material.

That's why living in an apartment with not a stick of furniture was so vitally important to her plan.

Luckily, the landlord had relented on the security deposit and had even given her a deep discount on the rent because he didn't like to have any of the apartments empty. Of course, that meant that the minute a real renter showed up, she and Tommy would be back out on the streets, but Clarissa hoped she'd have a diamond on her left ring finger before it came to that.

Under a blazing chandelier that had been put up by the previous tenants, Clarissa studied her palm. Sometimes she could see the tiny fork in the lines of her flesh. Sometimes she couldn't. But Sabrina had been very persuasive and she had the facts on her side.

Clarissa had been poor, hungry and had failed, or had been failed, in love already.

Clarissa had been tired and cold and without a place to call her own many times in her life. And she had a young son who relied on her and her alone.

But Clarissa also had a strength, a rock hard determination that Tommy would have a good life, that he wouldn't have to go through all the suffering she had endured.

Those were the facts and the future was up to Clarissa.

As Tommy said, if she was going to marry, why not choose a millionaire?

Clarissa winced, thinking of how cold and calculating it all sounded. She had grown up believing in love at first sight, in two lovers' destiny, in long deep kisses, and in promises that meant for always.

On the other hand, what had those beliefs ever gotten her? Other women, all through the centuries, chose their mates carefully, with an eye to the future, with an eye to how well that mate would provide for them and their children. Why shouldn't Clarissa learn a little calculation?

The security buzzer saved her from having to examine these notions too closely.

She rose and padded to the front hallway where the security system blinked.

"Who is it?" she asked, pressing the button on the intercom.

"A gentleman to see you," the doorman answered. "A Mr. Conor James."

Clarissa searched her memory.

Conor James? She had met a lot of wealthy men during the past couple of weeks, had had dinner with several of them, though nothing had ever gone further because she wasn't looking for an affair and many men were. And because she always made clear, right from the start, that she had a son. Lots of men wanted nothing to do with a woman with kids.

In fact, one of the things she liked about Fred Tannenbaum was that he didn't flinch when she mentioned Tommy. She liked it, and yet it made her feel even more guilty about regarding the man as a prize to be won or a goal to be accomplished.

But Conor James? The name sure didn't sound familiar.

"What does he want?" Clarissa asked.

"He says if you still want that hamburger, he's hungry, too."

Hamburger?

Oh, no.

That man. Clarissa groaned.

Trouble!

Danger!

Exactly the kind of man she could fall for, would fall for. Handsome. Smart-mouthed. Sexier than a man had a right to be. And just cocky enough to know it.

She shook her head.

On the other hand, she was hungry. The canapés at the reception had been dainty and less than filling. When Fred Tannenbaum invited her to join him for dinner, she had declined, because Whitney Bloomer, ace baby-sitter, had to study for an algebra quiz the next morning.

So a few sips of champagne, a triangle of pastry and a spoonful of caviar had been her dinner. And the only thing in her refrigerator was a corsage for tomorrow night's reception at the Art Institute, a week-old doggy bag from the Pump Room, and a bowl of congealing macaroni and cheese left over from Tommy and Whitney's dinner.

"Hamburger?" Tommy asked, coming into the hallway. "Did he say hamburger?"

Clarissa looked over at her son. "You should be in

bed," she warned. "Besides, this man is not somebody we want to be involved with. He's trouble."

"But will he buy us hamburgers?" Tommy persisted. "We don't have to date him. I mean, you don't
have to date him."

She studied her son. He seemed so excited by the
idea. It had been a long time since he had been excited
by something.

Maybe just this once...

"All right, but we're getting back home by ten and
you're going right to sleep," Clarissa warned. "And
that's only if he takes us both. We're a package deal,
right?"

"Yes, ma'am," he said with a mock salute that
made Clarissa smile.

"Tell him I'll be down in just a moment," Clarissa
said, punching down on the security button. "But ask
him whether he's willing to buy a second one for my
son."

Clarissa and Tommy looked at each other while
they waited for an answer. Having always been close
to her son, she knew exactly what her son was thinking.

Boy that hamburger's going to taste good!

Clarissa sighed. *I've got ten dollars—this week's
lunch money—if this character says he won't buy,* she
thought. *I could take Tommy around the corner after
I'm sure Conor James has walked away.*

The intercom crackled its reply.

"The gentleman says that's fine with him," the
doorman said.

"Yiippeee!" Tommy shrieked. "I'll go get dressed!"

Clarissa pulled her hair back in a scrunchie, yanked on her jeans and shoved her feet into her familiar cowboy boots. When mother and son came downstairs, she nodded at the doorman and swallowed as she saw Conor leaning against the delicately scrolled door.

Denim and boots. And a rakish smile.

Trouble, Clarissa groaned, trouble. She should turn right around and go back upstairs. But there was Tommy.

She squared her shoulders and took her son's hand in her own.

"This is Tommy," she said. "I'm Clarissa."

"One of the McShaunessy nieces, right?" Conor said, holding his hand out to high-five Tommy.

Clarissa was puzzled by his reference to nieces, but let it pass. She had more important concerns.

"You're buying, right?" she asked Conor, as soon as she was out of earshot of the doorman.

"Yeah," Conor said, sounding baffled. "You're my guests."

"Fine, then let's go to Hamburger Hamlet. I'll take one of their big burgers. With the works. And fries."

"Me, too!" Tommy said. "And an ice-cream soda afterward. If you wouldn't mind, that is."

"Whoa," Conor held up his hands. "What if I had said I wasn't buying?"

"Then Tommy and I would walk right back upstairs and go back to bed."

"You've got your own money," Conor said, jerking

his head back toward the elegant apartment building.
"Why does it matter so much whether I'm buying?"

"It just does."

"Wouldn't you buy me a hamburger?"

"No way."

"You sound a little like Scrooge."

"I give as much money to the charities as I can, I
pay my taxes like everyone else, I..."

"But you wouldn't buy me a hamburger."

"You look pretty able-bodied to me. Do you have
a job?"

"Not in the usual way."

"Thought not," Clarissa murmured.

*Maybe it's a good thing I've turned my love life
over to Tommy and Sabrina*, she thought. *Because I
always manage to be attracted to the men who need
me to take care of them.*

If her stomach wasn't growling and if Tommy
wasn't galloping in front of them like a wild horse,
she would turn around and run.

"I'm warning you," she said. "After we eat, we're
going home. Some of us work in the morning. And
Tommy goes to school."

"Oh, you have a job?"

"Actually, I do," Clarissa said, bristling at his de-
risive tone. "I'm substitute teaching one of the second
grade classes at the Latin School. But Tommy's with
a different teacher."

"Nice school," Conor said. "Are you an alumna?"

"Actually, no," she said, but she bit her tongue
rather than admit that instead of going to the presti-

gious private school, she had been educated at a public school in her Bridgeport neighborhood.

Tommy would have better.

She would make it so.

"That's where Tommy goes," she said.

She almost added that she had taken the low-paying job because the administration waived the stiff tuition for its teachers' children. Unfortunately, the job would last only until the regular teacher got back from maternity leave. Hopefully, she'd be married by then.

"You do a lot of socializing for someone who's concerned about the work ethic," Conor observed.

"How would you know?" Clarissa asked. Then, suddenly added, "How did you know where I live?"

"I saw you and Tannenbaum when he drove you home," Conor confessed. "I followed you. It was only two blocks from the Club."

"You followed me!" Clarissa cried. "That's awful."

"What I thought was awful was how Tannenbaum kissed you good-night."

Clarissa blushed. "You saw him kiss me?"

"So did the doorman and a half-dozen people on the street," Conor pointed out. "And it was a pretty dismal excuse for a kiss."

"We had just met," Clarissa protested. "He was being a gentleman."

"That kiss was the mildest caress I've ever seen between two people who haven't vowed lifelong chastity. That's not how I would have kissed you…how I will kiss you."

"You seem pretty sure of yourself."

"Oh, I am. Because you are a woman with a mouth that needs to be kissed."

Clarissa self-consciously touched the swelled flesh of her mouth with the tips of her fingers. She could just imagine how he would have kissed her...how he will kiss her...?

She covertly studied his firm, proud mouth.

She swallowed.

Hard.

No, no, Clarissa, she admonished herself.

"You're not going to kiss me," she warned. "Just so you know. And one other thing. This is absolutely the last time I'm going out with you."

"Aren't you a hard woman!"

Clarissa nearly denied it, but maybe it was better for him to think that she was. He stopped her, held her chin in his hand.

"You look so soft and beautiful," he said, studying first her eyes and then the parted lips. "But maybe you're as tough as nails."

"I am," she lied, trembling at his touch. "Tough as nails, that is."

She pulled away from him and he relinquished her, though they both knew he didn't have to. She had looked into his eyes and, for a moment, she had thought she was lost in them. Like sapphires and steel, they were.

But she wasn't—absolutely wasn't—going to fall for a louse this time.

"Are you guys coming or not?" Tommy shrieked from the door of Hamburger Hamlet. "I'm starved!"

"You had better be glad we have a chaperon,"

Conor said, raking his cool blue eyes across her body in a way that made her feel naked. "Because I would be happy to test out how a gentleman kisses a woman he's just met. And I'd be happy to show you how a real man kisses a woman he's interested in."

"And you'd better be glad we have a chaperon," Clarissa said. "Because I wouldn't be out here if you weren't buying Tommy a hamburger."

Seemingly shaken by her vehemence, Conor followed Tommy and Clarissa into the restaurant. They were shown a table for three. Tommy ordered a soda with "lots of maraschino cherries" and Clarissa ordered a club soda.

Conor asked for a cup of coffee.

"Can I offer you some menus?" the waiter asked.

"Oh, no," Tommy said. "I know what I want. One of your big burgers, with American cheese, well-done, ketchup, mustard, relish, lettuce, tomatoes, pickles. Some coleslaw on the side. Oh, and some fries. And an ice-cream sundae. Chocolate. Extra cherries."

"I'll take the same," Clarissa added.

The waiter looked up from his notepad.

"Same, I guess," Conor said.

Tommy took out some crayons from a glass set in the middle of the table and began drawing a spaceship on the white paper that covered the elegant tablecloths. Conor took a yellow crayon and drew a moon for Tommy's spaceship.

"So, do you think I have a chance with your mom?" he asked, his eyes challenging Clarissa's purse-mouthed glare.

"Mom's going to marry a millionaire," Tommy

said matter-of-factly, shaking his head. "You don't look like a millionaire to me."

"Tommy, don't," Clarissa said sternly.

"Sorry, Mom," Tommy relented. He paused a moment then added softly, "But she is, you know. Going to marry a millionaire."

As the little boy drew aliens and astronauts, flying saucers and comets, Conor leaned back in his chair and studied Clarissa. She blushed fiercely, her scattered freckles darkened, her amber eyes flashed—

Like fire.

Making love to her would be like catching a flame, he thought. Almost worth all the hassles.

And yet, like ice.

"Marrying a millionaire," he repeated coolly. "Guess that accounts for why a guy like me doesn't stand a chance."

"You're right," Tommy said, without looking up. "Unless, of course, you really are a millionaire."

Clarissa bit her lip. Though she had been a knockout in red, she was even more exciting with no makeup, Conor thought. More bed-ready. Made a man want to reach across the table and take her...

"You wouldn't understand," she said. "About the millionaire part."

"Try me," Conor challenged. "I've met plenty of women who wanted a man with money. You just want a man in your own class. What I can't figure out is why you're setting your sights on a mere millionaire. After all, you've got your own money, a nice place in the city. So a million here or a million there isn't going to make that much difference."

"But, we don't—" Tommy started.

Clarissa clapped a firm hand over her son's mouth. "Tommy, that's enough!" she warned.

The waiter reappeared with their drinks and Tommy tentatively sipped at his soda, holding it as if he expected it to be snatched from his hands at any moment. The adults warily regarded each other.

"So that's my problem. I don't measure up," Conor said, without rancor. "Financially, that is."

He didn't care. He had been given fair warning and though he would dearly love to bed this beautiful redhead once, maybe even more than once—he wouldn't demean himself, he couldn't demean himself by showing her his bank balance.

Clarissa closed her eyes.

"You don't understand," she repeated.

"No, I think I do understand."

"She has a plan," Tommy said. "She's going to marry a millionaire. And nothing less will do."

"And I'm sure nothing less should do," Conor said. He threw a few bills on the table. "Especially for you, Tommy. You really do deserve the very best. And if that means millionaire, good luck to your mom. Goodbye, pal."

And he walked out of the restaurant without another word.

Chapter Three

Third inning. Two outs. Kenny Mayfield at the plate. The air heavy with tension and anticipation.

Standing at the mound, Clarissa stared down Kenny Mayfield with narrowed eyes and a wry smile.

Then she blew her whistle.

"Kenny, tie your shoes," she said.

The second grader sheepishly looked down at his feet.

"Time-out!" he called.

Clarissa looked around the field and at Kenny's teammates, who lined up behind the batter's box for their turn. Thirty-two. Exactly right. Good.

Every few minutes for the past half hour, she recounted. Taking the second graders of Latin School to Lincoln Park to play kick ball was daunting. None of the regular teachers would do it—recess was usually games on the rooftop playground. But Clarissa often felt her energy was fed by the kids' enthusiasm. They loved going outside, the freedom of the grassy park, the moist, earthy air of breezes coming off Lake Michigan.

And so, after a productive morning of math, phonics

and cleaning the class turtle's aquarium, she had lined them up in twos. "Hold your partner's hand while we cross the street!" She had cried, repeating it as a mantra until she thought she would go hoarse.

And they crossed the street to the grassy fields. Clarissa felt wonderful—she had to admit, she was an outdoor kind of person, more comfortable with a carpet of grass and a ceiling that touched the sun. Maybe one day, she'd have a garden of her own, a little patch of lawn to mow.

Now, as she finished her count of the second graders, each and every one of them accounted for, she groaned.

There was an extra one.

From beyond left field, she saw him. Tall, lanky, a jean jacket thrown over his shoulder. Staring directly at her from under black wavy locks.

Conor James.

A catch in her throat, she purposefully turned and rolled the big red ball to Kenny. He missed. Strike!

When Conor James had walked out of the Hamburger Hamlet the night before, she had displayed no reaction in front of her son. And yet, inside, she had felt oddly bereft. As she and Tommy had walked back to the apartment after their sundaes, she had found herself searching the sidewalk for a glimpse of him.

Silly, she knew.

And yet, now as her heart raced, she knew that she had been feeling a little deflated ever since.

Worse than silly, she decided.

Angry at herself, she once again pitched the red ball down the alley of dirt and grass.

Kenny screwed up his face and kicked. His classmates erupted in cheers. The ball arched over the third base line, beyond outfielder Lisa Meyers, whose little legs pumped furiously as she raced to catch it.

Conor reached out with one hand and caught it.

"Out!" Lisa screamed. "He's out! It counts!"

Kenny, caught short at second, shrieked, "No!" but held the base, looking up uncertainly at Clarissa.

"Do over!" Clarissa announced.

Some kids groaned. Some clapped. Some muttered their complaints. Kenny skipped across the field to home.

Though her heart soared at the sight of him, Clarissa pursed her lips together as Conor crossed the third base line.

He threw the ball at her with an offhand shrug.

"Sorry I messed up the play," he said with a wicked grin that communicated he wasn't sorry. Not one little bit. He sat down on the bench next to Kenny's teammates.

"What are you doing here?" she asked, walking over to him.

"I happened to be in the neighborhood. I think it's a wonderful day, don't you?"

His easy smile invited agreement, but Clarissa shook her head.

"I'm working right now," she said distinctly. "I take my job very seriously. This is not talking time, this is work time."

She stopped herself as she noticed the stares of her class. *Oops,* she thought, *I'm talking to him as if he were a seven-year-old.* She started to smile, then caught herself as she saw the twinkle in his eye.

"Yes, teacher," he said with mock contrition. "I promise I'll be good."

Clarissa shook her head. She opened her mouth to tell him, right then and there, to leave her alone. Don't ever come back. Don't interfere with her life.

The Latin School bells tolled. The kids protested but obediently lined up for the return walk across the street to the stately Gothic elementary school building. Clarissa reminded them to find their partners. Michael refused to hold hands with Rosemary, claiming all girls had cooties. Lisa said she couldn't find her sweater. John said that Jeff's hands were too sweaty.

Saved by the bell.

Clarissa got the kids sorted out and led the double line across the field. Conor fell in beside her.

"I'm sorry about last night," he said. "I shouldn't have walked out on you two."

"It's okay," she said coolly. "We had a fine dinner without you. We took home a doggy bag and you still have $5.38 in change coming to you. I tip pretty big, because I have a soft spot for waiters."

"I wonder why."

"None of your business why. Give me your address, I'll mail you the change."

"I don't want my change, I want a chance to go out with you."

"Why? It's probably best that you walked out on me in the first place. I warned you that last night was absolutely—"

"I know. I know. Absolutely the last time you'd go out with me."

Conor threw his hands up in the air.

"So why do you want to see me?" Clarissa demanded.

"Because you're funny and smart and so beautiful it knocks my breath out," he said, exasperated. "And I couldn't get you out of my head last night even though I tried my absolute best. I counted sheep, and their wool turned red like the color of your hair. I stared out the window, but all the city lights sparkled like your eyes. I paced, but the sound reminded me of the click of your heels. I tried music, but every song seemed to be about you. Clarissa, I tried to get you out of my head. I can't."

Clarissa shook her head. She had tried to forget about him, too. And failed.

"That's not good enough," she said. Because it wasn't. Really wasn't.

"What wasn't good enough? How hard I tried?"

"No, not that. The reasons you give for wanting to see me aren't good enough."

He crimsoned as if she had slapped him.

"What more can a man do or say to get a chance with you?"

"Look, Conor, I'm thirty years old, I've got a seven-year-old son, I've got to think of my future. Our future. I won't, I won't…"

"Screw up by going out with a guy like me?"

"Yes, that's it exactly."

"So that means you'd like to. If you could afford to."

"That means...you're nice."

He smiled lazily, an insight suddenly coming to him.

"Ah, Clarissa, you're not very good at hiding the truth. You're very attracted to me. *Nice* is not the word you're thinking of."

She deftly ignored him by shooting to the head of the line to direct the children across the crosswalk. As the last pair got on the next block, Conor came up behind her.

"Admit it," he growled.

"All right, I admit it," Clarissa said, annoyed. "You're handsome and you're sexy and you're funny and bright. But I've only met you twice. I don't know anything about you. What I do know tells me that we don't have a future. And a man without a future isn't for me."

"No one-night stands, no flings, no whirlwind affairs? I've been told I'm worth it."

"No," Clarissa said firmly.

"And your husband has to be a millionaire."

She took a deep breath, and he pounced on her hesitation.

"Just millionaires, huh?" He prodded. "Oilmen, investment bankers, real estate developers—those are the men who make your heart go pitter-patter?"

"It's not that cold-blooded."

"It sounds pretty cold-blooded to judge a man's worth solely by his bank account. But maybe that's all you've grown up with. Money. Money. And more money. But there's more to a man. Much more. Maybe your finishing school didn't teach you that."

Clarissa bit her lip. Oh, how little he knew! Every day she said the same thing to herself at least six or seven times, it was cold-blooded, it was calculating, it was a strange way to approach marriage—to say the very least.

But she had a son who needed her to make tough choices, to be rational and to think hard about life.

She never wanted Tommy to see the inside of a homeless shelter again. She never wanted Tommy to go to bed hungry again. She never wanted him to feel the pain he felt when his father walked out on them, drunk and with another, *younger* woman. And never, ever would she let him live only on the charity of the state. She had to give him more. And she couldn't let her judgment in men get the better of her.

A millionaire. Her palm had the lines to prove it.

"I've made mistakes in my life relying on other indicators about a man," she said, her voice a bare whisper.

He looked her up and down. It was tough not to see her as a strong but very fragile woman. He couldn't bring himself to judge her.

And yet, the men she was so quick to dismiss—they were just like him. Or what he used to be. The carpenters, the electricians, the cabdrivers, the cops. The workingman, who was a hero for getting up every morning to do a job. The workingman, who was wealthy but maybe not in the way that padded his wallet.

Still, he could see her pain was real. Very real.

"I'm sorry to hear that," he said simply.

The children lined up in front of the door to the Latin School. Clarissa turned one last time to Conor.

"Work a little harder at forgetting me," she said. "Because I'm not seeing you again. You don't have a job, you don't have a suit—"

"Whoa, there, how do you know I don't have a job?"

Clarissa sighed.

"First of all, you virtually admitted it last night. And second, it's Tuesday at eleven o'clock in the morning," she said. "And you don't have anywhere you have to be. Figure it out."

She turned on her heels and trotted to the front of the line of kids, counting them quickly in her head. Thirty-two. All present and accounted for. She put her key card into the door of the school and opened it, assigning two children to be the door holders for their classmates.

"One other thing!" Conor called from the sidewalk. "How do you know I don't own a suit?"

She ushered the last pair of children into the door and shot him a dismissive look.

"Because everyone knows you don't go to the University Club without a suit and tie. You should have worn a suit. You didn't fit in."

She closed the door behind her without a backward glance.

"I don't always want to," he called after her.

"HEY, YOU DEADBEAT, get on up here!"

Conor looked up at the top spire of the Gothic Latin

building. His friend Bill, bald as an elf, hung out the window, waving a wrench with false menace.

"Took you long enough to get here," he scolded.

"I did my best," Conor said. "I left the house as soon as I got your call. I just got...delayed."

Conor's smile gave away nothing, yet Bill had been his friend for so long that there was no fooling him.

"Ha! I knew it. It was girl trouble."

Conor shook his head. "I'm too old for that playboy stuff."

"You're more of a playboy than I'll ever be," Bill replied. "Now stop chitchatting and get up here—if you worked for me, I'd dock your pay."

"If I worked for you, you'd have to pay me in the first place."

Conor took the interior stairs two at a time to the third floor. He was very tempted, but disciplined himself not to make a side trip to the second grade classroom.

Gold digger.

He had met plenty of them in his time. Enough that he could be forgiven if he no longer sympathized with the treasure seekers.

Serves her right if she ends up with Tannenbaum, Conor thought. Nothing bad about Tannenbaum, nice enough guy and all.

But so very boring...

On the other hand, he'd give her what she wanted. Diamonds. Furs. Designer clothes. Luxury cars. Travel to exotic locales. Pampering. Her every whim indulged.

That's what she wanted, more of the same of what she had.

And yet, though he had never heard a woman be so straightforward about her matrimonial intentions, he got the feeling Clarissa McShaunessy didn't really know what she wanted.

Otherwise, how could he explain the way she looked at him just moments ago? How could he explain the way her lower lip trembled when he touched her? Or the way the back of her neck arched when he had whispered those first words in her ears at the party for Tannenbaum?

One other thing puzzled him.

Who was she and why had they only just now met?

Working his way up from south side Irish laborer to skilled carpenter to contractor to developer, he had started out with nothing but the clothes on his back to owning a few buildings on the city's north side and finally he now possessed entire blocks of Chicago. He had met many wealthy and sophisticated women of the very best families. Some he had courted, some had chased after him, and though he was regarded as "new" money, he was still enticing enough to be invited to their parties and receptions and dinners.

On the third floor, he entered a children's art studio. Finger paintings hung from clotheslines strung between the walls. Sunlight streamed through the tissue paper mosaics taped to the windows. On the butcher-block worktables were scattered clay sculptures rivaling the best Conor had seen in the finest private collections of modern artwork. The studio smelled of paste and Play-Doh.

Bill stuck his head out from under a large white ceramic sink.

"I don't know how many times I've told those teachers that when the kids make macaroni necklaces, they can't let them shove the pasta down the sink," he complained. "They think it's a game, but the stuff expands when it's wet and completely destroys the pipes. Get under here and help."

The two men worked together for several minutes under the sink before the bell rang announcing the beginning of third period.

Conor, lying under the sink, lifted his head to see thirty young faces staring solemnly at him and Bill. And beyond them Clarissa stood at the light switch.

"So that's girl trouble," Bill whispered, putting down his wrench long enough to ogle Clarissa. "If she's what caused the delay, Conor, I don't blame you."

"She's not our type," Conor said under his breath. "Old money."

"Old money, huh! That's definitely not us. You're new money and I'm no money."

Clarissa broke apart the mass of children and came up to the sink. She stared down at the two men.

"Does this mean we shouldn't have art class this morning?" She asked, pointedly directing her question to Bill.

"Uh, you wouldn't want to," Bill answered, gulping air. "Give us another half hour."

Clarissa smiled winningly.

"We'll do math first and come back next period."

Bill sat up, banging his head into the bottom of the

sink as he did. The pain meant nothing to him. He stared openmouthed as Clarissa lined up the children and explained that they would walk single file back downstairs to their classroom. Conor slid out from under the sink and wiped his hands on a nearby rag.

As the last child left the room, Clarissa looked back.

"Does Conor work for you?" she asked Bill.

Bill recovered some of his composure.

"Him? Oh, no," he said, looking at Conor and recovering his impish humor. "I'd never have him work for me. He's too lazy. And late. Always late. He's just helping me out this morning. If he's lucky, I'll feed him dinner tonight."

"I didn't think he had a job," Clarissa said crisply.

She said goodbye to the two of them and slammed the door shut behind herself.

"Wow, she's beautiful," Bill said. "If I wasn't married and didn't have three kids and—"

"She's a gold digger," Conor interrupted sharply.

"So? That means you two are a perfect match. She's digging for gold and you're fourteen karats."

"Yeah, but I don't like women who like me for my money."

"Then it's even better—she's probably the only woman in Chicago who doesn't know you're loaded. I think I just gave her the impression that you're unemployed. And lazy, too. Sorry about that, buddy."

"Doesn't matter. She won't give me the time of day. Because she doesn't know."

"So then, tell her."

"If I did that, she'd just be with me because I measured up on a bank balance."

Bill shook his head and went back to work under the sink.

"You make it too hard on yourself, buddy," he said. "You shoulda been like me. Gotten married straight out of school. I mean, you remember those last few months we spent horsing around before we got all responsible? Man, the girls were so beautiful that summer..."

Bill continued to ruminate aloud on the summer they graduated as he worked. Eighteen years ago. The music was better. The beer was better—none of this fancy microbrewery stuff for Bill, he liked his cold, American and in a frosty mug. And the food was better—a man could get a hamburger without somebody trying to put sprouts on it or lecture him about cholesterol. And the girls? The girls were fantastic—not that he wouldn't marry his wife Katie in an instant if he had it to do all over again.

As Bill talked, Conor felt a wave of nostalgia—and a nudge of his memory. There had been a girl, a redhead, at the SummerFest. He could nearly conjure up the exact hue of gold and burgundy. But nothing else.

Still, he could call up the feeling she had evoked—a girl he had never even spoken to, whom he had never again seen. A feeling of being understood, of someone else facing the world as he did. With a fighting optimism, a cheeky kind of determination against overwhelming odds.

He wondered if he had been attracted to Clarissa because she reminded him of that girl, of that feeling he had that summer so long ago.

Clarissa McShaunessy, niece of the Baltimore

McShaunessy dynasty, wouldn't understand those feelings. Clarissa McShaunessy had probably faced tragedies no more daunting than a broken nail or a ten percent dip in the stock market eating into her trust fund.

"That's the last of it," Bill said, finishing his trip down memory lane just as he squeezed the last nut into place. "These pipes will have to last until the next disaster."

"We're done?"

"Yeah, thanks for the help. Wanna ride downtown? I got the pickup."

"No, thanks, I'm going to walk."

The two men said goodbye after making plans for a working lunch the next day in Bridgeport. Conor had already persuaded Bill to take on all the plumbing work for his proposed renovation of a central block in the neighborhood. Although *persuaded* was a very funny term when the job represented more money than Bill had made in all the ten years since he bought his father's plumbing business.

Conor slipped out the back staircase of the building, certain he didn't want to accidentally run into Clarissa.

On the sidewalk, he tucked his hands in the pockets of his worn and weathered jeans. He fit into them as perfectly as he had when he was twenty. These jeans, washed in corner laundromats and laundered by well-paid housekeepers at various times in his life, were his only link to the world he worked his way out of.

These jeans were forgiven by those who knew—whose knowledge of the movers and shakers of Chicago was precise and accurate. Who knew that Conor never wore a suit.

He figured he had solved the mystery of his attraction to Clarissa. She simply reminded him of someone else. Now that he knew, he wouldn't have to think of her again. Conor was glad to have resolved that problem.

Because one thing he was certain of: he and Clarissa could never come together. After all, if she couldn't accept the kind of man he had been, he couldn't share with her the man he was.

Besides, he'd never liked snobs.

Chapter Four

"Would you like some more champagne?" Fred Tannenbaum inquired, pulling the bottle from the ice bucket which had been placed next to their table.

He had taken a chance, canceling some late meetings to make a date with her. It had been a simple matter to get her phone number, but harder to entice her to join him. The excitement he had felt when she said yes made him worry at the very same time he celebrated his good fortune.

How could his feelings depend on a woman he had only met a couple of days ago?

"No, thank you, one glass of this wonderful stuff is my limit," Clarissa said, shaking her head. He noticed she was careful not to displace any of the crystal pins used to secure her hair—she wore a style that made a man itch to reach out and touch.

Whoever did her hair had outdone himself this afternoon, using Clarissa's flame-haired beauty as the perfect palette. Fred also noted the women in surrounding tables openly appraising Clarissa. He guessed the diamond-studded hairpins would be "the look" within days.

As if any woman could look quite like Clarissa.

Clarissa wore a hot pink chiffon scarf and a black velvet sheath. Her sophisticated image was complete with a rich ruby shade of lipstick and a daub of perfume Fred thought he recognized as Chanel. Fred Tannenbaum loved a woman who knew how to pull out all the stops on glamour, but he also appreciated a down-home heart.

He sensed both in Clarissa, and he was beginning to think he had met his match. He certainly felt younger and stronger than he had felt in a long, long time.

"Perhaps more caviar?"

"No, thank you, Fred. But, please, you have some. And tell me more about the ranch."

Her polite, encouraging smile gave her face a special glow. He knew she wouldn't like to hear it, but the scattering of freckles on her nose deepened in color, giving her a pixieish quality.

Oh, how Fred Tannenbaum loved having a beautiful woman at his table.

He loved it when men cast looks—part envy, part sheer admiration—in his direction. He even liked the stares of other women, whose estimation of his prowess naturally shot up when he escorted a beauty.

A small vanity, perhaps, but one that had comforted him greatly in the years since the death of his beloved wife June. If June was still alive, there would be no other women. June had always been beauty enough for him. Even—no, especially—after twenty years of marriage.

But for many long lonely years now he had had to make do without her.

Although he knew making do when you're the CEO of one of the largest, most profitable oil companies in the country wasn't really so bad. He'd had starlets, fashion models, heiresses, artists and society women to keep him company. All of them years younger than himself, all beautiful, all eager to please, all conscious of the Tannenbaum name and worth. Right down to the penny.

Clarissa was all of the above, but so much more.

She was beautiful—though many would argue that her delicate features and long flame-ridden curls belonged to the romanticism of nineteenth century poets and artists. She was eager, had sought him out at the University Club party and had clearly done her homework about himself and his business. And she couldn't have done that homework without being conscious of the Tannenbaum name and his money.

Yet, there was something different about her—a warmth and an honesty, an innocence and an earnestness.

He could ask her to marry him.

And she would say yes.

What a surprising notion! he thought as he sipped his champagne and joined her in watching the rain pelt the windows of the LaTour Restaurant.

He hadn't considered the idea of a second marriage before, though certainly the society page of nearly every metropolitan newspaper had speculated about him. He had topped many ten most eligible bachelor lists, even though he didn't do half the things gossip columnists thought he did.

He told another anecdote about his ranch adventures and she laughed at all the right places. He suspected he wasn't quite as interesting as she made him feel, but he couldn't be blamed if a glass of champagne and a beautiful woman made him talkative.

"Perhaps some dessert before we go?" he asked.

She had left a mouthful of champagne in her glass, and her attention, ordinarily so focused on him, tripped elsewhere.

Sometimes Fred wanted to follow.

He took the bottle from the hovering waiter and poured another glass for himself.

"Penny for your thoughts," he said, realizing he really didn't know very much about this beauty. "Or perhaps I should offer more?"

Clarissa startled and her amber eyes widened. Fred felt a stab of desire. He wondered when it would be time to touch her. Not too soon, because he recognized she wasn't that kind of woman. She lived at the very finest address and although she had firmly put off his inquiries, he guessed she must come from a very old, very wealthy, very proper Chicago family.

A man didn't bed a woman like that and give her a few baubles from Tiffany's when he was tired of her.

No, wealthy families protected their women from dangerous men. He hadn't inquired but he was sure that if he asked the right questions, he would find out that there was an uncle who owned a bank or a father who headed an investment outfit—and that instead of a duel fought for her honor, there would be a business retaliation if he toyed with Clarissa's heart.

On the other hand, it was agony to go out with her, to be near her and not touch her. She had awakened in him passions and urgencies he thought were gone forever. And in just two days!

"I'm sorry, Fred, I've been distracted," she said. "I was...I was feeling guilty."

"Guilty? I don't think I've ever heard a woman confess to that particular emotion in twenty years. Didn't you know that guilt was something that went out with poodle skirts?"

She smiled at his teasing.

"I feel guilty about us," she confessed soberly.

"About us?" Fred inquired coolly. He wondered what catastrophic turn this conversation might take.

"I haven't been completely honest with you. Or completely fair."

Fred inwardly recoiled, though he was too much of a hardened businessman and negotiator to let his feelings show.

"And you've told me a naughty little lie?" he asked with false nonchalance.

Her face blushed a delicate pink and Fred chuckled with relief.

My God, he thought, she's the real article, a woman with scruples, a woman who really feels that old-fashioned emotion—guilt. Something to accompany her timeless looks.

"Oh, I think I can figure this out," he said, trying to put her at ease. "You're wondering whether it's all right to see me even if, were I poor, you wouldn't see me at all.''

She swallowed. Her delicate shoulders shivered so slightly. Fred was touched. And so relieved that her qualms were about nothing more troubling. He had heard of men losing their families, their honor, their businesses over beauties without such moral qualms.

He wondered what proper and wealthy family brought her up with such honorable ideas.

"It's all right, Clarissa," he reassured her. "I'm the ultimate realist. I'm wealthy. You're a beauty with money of her own. We wouldn't see each other if it were any different. If it weren't for my money, I'd just be an ordinary man on the wrong side of forty. Maybe a little rougher around the edges than most. I'd never have a chance with you."

He crossed his fingers under the table as he wondered whether she knew he was actually closing in on fifty. Few people did. His press releases made sure of that.

"That doesn't bother you?" Clarissa asked. "The money part?"

"Not at all," Fred said smoothly. "I've become very at ease with my money—not many people are. Now, if you don't want any more champagne, should we get your wrap and head for the symphony? The concert's starting in a half hour."

HE HAD ONLY GOTTEN IT half right, Clarissa thought as she pulled the vintage black velvet cape around her shoulders. She watched from the warmth of LaTour's lobby as Fred stood in the chilly rain to signal his driver.

Sure, she had doubts about going out with him. About his money. Or rather, about whether she would want to be with him if he had none and if that meant that she shouldn't be with him if he had any. The doubt and the guilt she had carried with her every second since she had held her palm out to Sabrina for her fortune.

But those feelings, while constant, were quelled by images that reminded her that she didn't have the luxury to turn back on the plan to marry a millionaire.

The images were harsh—the long lines at the homeless shelter, the feel of Tommy's ribs as he slept in her arms on the narrow cot, the job applications that asked all the same questions and answered all the same way—sorry, not hiring right now, come back in six months. And her own frustration—*I can't wait six months to get a job to feed my son.*

No, dating Fred Tannenbaum was not wrong. He was nice and friendly. Sweet, really. And rich as all get-out. She knew herself well enough to know that she would always treat him well.

But dating Fred while dreaming of Conor James was an entirely different matter.

Watching Fred as the rain battered his tuxedo jacket, she could just kick herself—although in her four-inch heels, she'd probably land on her butt if she did.

Why, oh why, was her mind, her dreams, her energies, focused on an unemployed louse who couldn't even afford a second pair of jeans? Conor James, no-account. She had done her best to push thoughts of him away, but she had felt his presence everywhere.

As if his scent, of pine and citrus, was on her.

She was supposed to be focused on how to marry a millionaire.

Her own palm had better taste in men than her brain or her heart did.

"Clarissa! Come on," Fred called, waiting at the rented limousine. The doorman opened the restaurant's heavy glass door for her.

Pulling her wrap around her shoulders to block the wet autumn wind, she walked out onto the sidewalk, self-conscious at the stares she provoked from people gathered under the awning for protection from the storm.

"Isn't she the one that's in that movie?" one woman demanded of her companion. "What's her name? I can't think of it."

As people weighed in on some names, Clarissa turned her head, thinking she could catch a glimpse of a real star. But as her eyes met those of the people crouched against the building to avoid the pelting rain, she realized they thought she was the celebrity.

Although exactly which one was in some doubt.

She blanched at the attention, but when she turned back to Fred's safe, waiting arms, she caught sight of a single man leaning against the marble facade of the restaurant. Jeans soaked, leather jacket opened to reveal a wet T-shirt, hair slicked back, face nearly, but not completely, in shadow.

Clarissa's heart lurched.

His mocking eyes met hers.

She pursed her lips in a disdain she didn't feel.

That man. Conor James. Just as she had resolved to put thoughts of him aside. And hadn't she told him, just this morning, that he should stay away from her?

He smiled knowingly, his lips full and proud. And then he gestured, so slightly only she would notice the tilt of his head, towards Fred and the waiting car.

As if to say, you've made your bargain with fortune, now you have to pay the price.

She tilted her chin resolutely and whirled around to get into the limo.

"Symphony Hall," Fred told the driver as he settled in beside Clarissa. "Darling, I'm having such a wonderful time. How 'bout you?"

Clarissa looked back once through the rain-splattered window. Conor was still there, leaning against the building, unmindful of the rain. Haunting her.

She turned, biting her lip until she could taste the blood.

"I'm having a wonderful time," she said emphatically.

BACK AT THE LaTour Restaurant, the maître d' apologized once more and offered Conor a snifter of Grand Marnier, which he declined.

"I'm sorry the doorman failed to recognize you," he said for the third time. "If he had seen you, he would have immediately brought out an umbrella. No need for you to stand on the sidewalk in the rain."

"Armand, relax," Conor said. "I wanted to stand there for a little while."

"But we like to keep our preferred customers happy."

"I'm glad I'm preferred, but you don't have to worry about me."

"Would you like a new shirt?" Armand offered. "I'm sure I can get a dry one for you from the all-night shop around the corner."

"Armand, go bother another preferred customer," Conor ordered good-naturedly. "I'm perfectly happy with my coffee."

The maître d' withdrew discreetly.

Although he had been courteous and friendly to Armand, Conor was in a foul mood. It wasn't the wet jeans and the soaked boots. He'd lived with worse many times when working construction—and he'd learned to like it if it was for his own business.

No, what made him so miserable was a woman.

That woman.

An admitted gold digger, at that.

His eyes narrowed as he thought of the woman he could have if he was honest with her. But wasn't sure if he could respect her if she knew the truth.

THE NEXT EVENING, Tommy thoughtfully stared at his mom, who sat on the bed in an ivory one-shouldered dress. No shoes. No makeup. Hair in a ponytail. To his eyes, she looked like a goddess.

"I could baby-sit myself," he offered. Whitney Bloomer, the older sister of one of his classmates, had been grounded for getting a C on her algebra quiz. If Tommy had known what algebra was, he would have studied it himself just so he could help Whitney to get a better grade.

Clarissa shook her head.

"I could do it!" he challenged. "You could lay out my dinner. I would eat it, take my dishes back to the kitchen counter, watch television until seven o'clock, brush my teeth, read myself a good-night story…" His voice trailed off as he realized his sales job wasn't working.

"I'd really rather stay home with you anyhow," Clarissa said. "We could play cards. I'll make you brownies. Caramel pecan, your favorite."

"That's not how you're going to get a husband," Tommy said, crossing his arms in front of his chest. "Mr. Tannenbaum has a very important dinner this evening with his new partners. He'll want you there. Remember—dating is dress rehearsal for marriage. This dinner is when you can show him that you're a good hostess."

"How did you get so sophisticated, knowing about dating?" Clarissa asked. As Tommy drew himself up to explain, she raised her hand. "Don't tell me, Tommy. I wouldn't want to know. You're too worldly as it is."

The doorbell rang. Tommy slipped his mother's evening bag out from under the twin bed and padded out to the hallway to hit the security buzzer, signaling to the doorman that it was all right to send up their visitor.

"That'll be Mr. Tannenbaum," he said. "You get dressed. I'll talk to him. I wanted to ask him a little about the oil business anyhow."

Clarissa shook her head.

"You're not staying here on your own," she said. "I'm staying home tonight and frankly, I'm going to love it. I'm not really the dating type and going out every night is a little tiring."

"If you're just worried about quality time, forget it," Tommy said, opening the front door and watching for the elevator. "You spend more time with me than most moms."

"I'd like a real home life," Clarissa mused.

She hadn't wanted him to hear that, but the words had slipped out before she thought. He pounced on the chance to tell her again the virtues of marrying a millionaire.

"Once you marry Tannenbaum, we'll have a real family," he said. "And you'll stay home every night."

"And when is the wedding?" A deep voice asked.

Tommy and Clarissa startled as Conor walked into the open door. He smiled with equal good-naturedness at Clarissa and Tommy both, ignoring Clarissa's open-mouthed stare.

"Hi, there, sport," he said to Tommy. He nodded at Clarissa.

"What are you doing here?" she asked, eyes narrowing. She had recovered from her shock at seeing him, here in the flesh, after a night spent trying her best to erase his image from her mind. The nerve of the man! Walking in here where he had no right.

"I came by to tell you a few things about myself that you ought to know before you go chasing after millionaires..." He stopped himself, looking beyond the barren hallway to the empty living room. "Say, where's the furniture?"

"It's being cleaned," Tommy said smoothly. "Every piece of furniture is being cleaned. By professional cleaners. We send it all out twice a year."

The two males stared at each other.

"Haven't you ever heard of that?" Tommy demanded. "All the best families do it that way. We send the staff on a vacation at the same time. That's why I answered the door this evening."

Clarissa looked up at the Baroque-corniced ceiling. Tommy was laying it on a little thick. But Conor wouldn't know the difference, would he?

He looked as if he had more important things on his mind than figuring out why she didn't have any furniture.

"Clarissa, I'm here to tell you the truth about myself because I decided last night that it doesn't matter if you would want me for my—"

"We've already covered this," Clarissa reminded him. "But you don't seem to understand that the truth about you doesn't matter. What's important is—"

"Hey, wait a minute!" Tommy interrupted. "Mr. James, you don't have a job, do you?"

"Well, not in the usual sense."

"That's what my Dad used to say all the time," Tommy said dismissively. "But have you got references?"

"Why are you asking?"

"Because my mom's about to offer you a job."

"She is?"

"I am?"

"Yes. Baby-sitting me. Starting now. Give us a list of your references," Tommy said brazenly. "She's got to call them right now. Don't be shy, she'll give you a decent hourly wage, I'm pretty self-sufficient, and, from the looks of you, it might be the first honest money you've earned in months."

Chapter Five

"Conor James? I've known him for years. Greatest guy in the world," Mr. Smith, headmaster of the Latin School, said over the phone. "Go on out this evening. Have a wonderful time. Conor will take care of Tommy just fine. You don't need to worry a bit."

Clarissa held the telephone more tightly and looked out into the living room where Conor and Tommy sat on the floor playing checkers.

The domesticity of the scene made her throat clutch, even if it was in a room with none of the usual touches of home. Not even a single stick of furniture. Would she always live in empty rooms? Would she ever give Tommy a better life? How about a father who would play board games with him, who would spend time with him, who wouldn't run out on him?

Was Fred that man?

Did it have to be a millionaire?

Well, whoever she married, he'd have to be a solid citizen.

"He says he doesn't have a regular job!" Clarissa wailed at the headmaster.

Roderick Smith laughed aloud.

"I guess nothing Conor James has ever done can be called 'regular,'" he conceded. "And if that's how he wants to explain what he does, who am I to contradict him? But you should know that the finest Chicago families wouldn't think twice about leaving their children with him. Although why Conor would get into the baby-sitting business, I can't imagine."

I can just imagine, Clarissa thought to herself. He's agreed to be a baby-sitter because he can't keep a regular job.

"If you don't mind my asking, how did you meet him?" she queried, hesitant to ask her boss, the head of the school, such a personal question over the phone. But she had to know before she left Tommy with him.

Why couldn't Whitney Bloomer have gotten a better grade in algebra?

"I don't mind telling you at all—he was in my freshman class at University of Chicago," Mr. Smith explained. "Poor guy was on scholarship, but the money dried up and he had to drop out. I think he was a carpenter then. But I understand he never got that diploma. And he didn't work as a carpenter for long, did he? Funny how people turn out, isn't it?"

Yes, Clarissa thought. Real funny. Some men took responsibility for their lives and their families and some men didn't.

A woman would be a fool to hitch her wagon to a man whose prospects—she stopped herself.

Conor wasn't asking for a future.

No, he was just asking for a one-night stand, a little fun, a cheap affair and then—Clarissa was sure—out the door and onto his next conquest.

Yeah, it was funny how some men had responsibility written all over them, and some men were just...

"You're right, it is funny," Clarissa murmured.

She glanced at her watch. Seven-thirty.

Had to make a decision. Go or don't go. She'd give anything for just a quiet evening at home with Tommy. But if she wanted a ring from Fred Tannenbaum, she had better get her act together.

Playing hostess at a dinner party for his new partners at the finest restaurant in town was, just as Tommy said, like an audition for her as Fred's wife.

She wanted to win the role.

The headmaster must have heard her troubled sigh.

"If you don't mind my asking you a personal question...Clarissa, have I heard correctly that you're seeing Fred Tannenbaum?"

Clarissa took a deep breath, shoving down all her ethical misgivings. She marveled at how quickly news traveled in the small, tightly knit upper reaches of Chicago society.

"Yes," she said, and quickly added. "But I promise nothing will interfere with my work until Mrs. Frehe comes back from maternity leave."

Mr. Smith repeated that Conor would make a fine baby-sitter, and thanked her again for taking on the second grade class on such short notice. As if giving her a job when she was down to her last dollar were a favor to him.

For the hundredth time, she silently thanked Sabrina for the recommendation for the job. Sabrina's daughter had been working as a nurse's aide at the hospital where Mrs. Frehe had delivered. Latin School was just one of the many job leads Clarissa had followed up—but it was clearly the best, giving her a good educational atmosphere for Tommy and helping her appear to all who met her as a wealthy young single mom who worked out of boredom instead of need. If only she could have confided in Hallie and Maggie about the changes in her life...

Shoving aside her longings, she made her second call.

"Conor James? Baby-sitting?" The gruff voice erupted in laughter. "You've got to be kidding me. Is this some kind of practical joke that he put you up to? 'Cause I wouldn't put it past him. Baby-sitting. Now that's something new. I think I've heard everything."

"It's not a joke, and I'm sorry to bother you, but I need to know if it's all right to leave my son with him," Clarissa explained.

Though she didn't know Bill O'Neill, she had seen the young plumbing contractor at Latin school enough to trust that he would tell her the truth. On the other hand, this conversation wasn't going as well as she would have liked.

"Conor's going into the baby-sitting business?"

"Yes, I'm going out this evening...on a date and my son needs a baby-sitter," she explained further, assuming perhaps that he simply had been startled by her call.

"Why?"

"Why what?"

"Why would you go out with someone else if Conor was there?"

"I...well, I've already made plans with my...my

gentleman friend. And Conor has agreed to baby-sit,''
Clarissa said, feeling as though this conversation were
going around in circles.

A long, excruciating silence followed.

"You aren't by any chance a redhead, are you?"

"Well, yes, I am."

Bill whistled. "Boy, Conor's got it bad. Real bad."

Clarissa stared heavenward. This conversation was
starting to sound like something from *Alice's Adventures in Wonderland!*

"Just tell me, is he reliable?"

"Conor, yeah, he's reliable. And rich or poor, he's
a wonderful guy."

"The reliability part is all I needed to know," Clarissa said. "Thank you so much for the recommendation."

As she hung up the phone, Conor looked up from
the checkers game.

"Did my references check out okay?" he asked sardonically.

"As a matter of fact, they did," Clarissa said. "Although your friend Bill is a bit weird."

Conor shrugged. "That's not the worst thing that's
been said about him."

Clarissa walked over to the checkers board and
crouched down next to her son.

The high slit of her dress fell open, exposing long,
bare legs. Conor's eyes skittered over her, and though
her son remained utterly oblivious, the sexual electricity in the air was unmistakable.

She tugged her dress about her, careful to keep the
white gossamer fabric from tearing.

"Shouldn't you be putting on your makeup?" Tommy asked. "You're beautiful, Mom, but you look a little flushed. A touch of powder would take care of that."

"You go find my makeup bag and my pumps," Clarissa said. "The shoes are in the bedroom—the gray ones. I have no idea where the makeup bag is."

As soon as Tommy was out of earshot, Clarissa leaned toward Conor. His musk and citrus scent might have had an effect on an ordinary woman, but Clarissa was no ordinary woman.

She was a mom, thinking about her child's safety.

"If anything happens to him while I'm gone, I'll track you down to the ends of the earth and rip you apart," she said in her sternest tone.

Then she leaned back on her heels, determined not to let his nearness distract her.

"If you talk like that to every baby-sitter, no wonder you can't keep anybody for long," Conor said blandly.

"I'm in a bind tonight because my regular baby-sitter got a C in algebra and she's grounded!"

"And you're very welcome," he replied with an implacable grin.

Clarissa growled in frustration just as she realized that she should say thank you to him since he was, after all, helping her out. On the other hand, he had all the markings of a man quite pleased with himself— so very arrogantly pleased with himself that she just couldn't bring herself to give him the satisfaction he wanted.

"Oh, maybe I just shouldn't go!" she exclaimed.

He caught her elbow and brought her face close to his. For one wild instant, she thought he was going to kiss her. But his touch wasn't sexual, it had a purpose. The purpose was to defend his manhood.

"Look, you might think I'm completely irresponsible because I don't put on a suit and tie and punch in at an office at nine every morning," Conor growled. "But I am an honorable man. I keep my promises. I honor the commitments I make. I take care of children, pets and other treasures entrusted to me."

"Really?" Clarissa said with as much coolness as she could muster.

"If you want to call Rod back, he'll tell you that I kept thirty-six iguanas in my apartment over Christmas break last year for the ninth grade science class," he added good-naturedly. "Not a single iguana lost, killed or otherwise harmed."

His eyes twinkled with mirth but brooked no contradiction. Embarrassed, she lowered her eyes. He let go of her elbow.

The security buzzer rang just as Tommy returned to the living room with a pair of heels and a tube of lipstick.

"All I could find was raspberry swirl," he complained.

"Go on," Conor said softly. "You can call the headmaster again, if you'd like. Or maybe I should give you the phone number of the mayor."

Clarissa shook her head. There was something about him, something in his eyes or maybe in the open but proud way he held himself. The satisfaction he sought now was acknowledgment of his honor. She could at least grant him that.

"All right, I believe you," she surrendered. "I have no idea why, but I do."

"Come on, Mom!" Tommy urged. "The dinner was supposed to begin a half hour ago and Tannenbaum's downstairs. Don't want to make him wait."

Clarissa slipped on her pumps and pulled the scrunchie out of her hair, letting long lush waves cascade loose down her back. No time now for real makeup, no time for an elaborate 'do, not even time for a quick spritz of one of the perfume samples she had stockpiled in the bathroom.

"You look wonderful," Tommy said, handing her the tube of lipstick. "I can hear wedding bells already."

She dabbed her mouth with the raspberry gloss and then checked her reflection in the sprawling living room window. From behind her, reflected from the long window, the twinkling lights of the city promised adventure, romance, possibilities....

She turned around to look at her son, who was already contemplating his next move on the board. Conor sat across from him, deep in thought as he stared at the pieces.

"Go on, Mom," Tommy said. "We'll be fine."

Looking up, Conor smiled lazily at her, and nodded toward the buzzer, which was ringing for a second, much more insistent, time.

"Don't keep the millionaire waiting," Conor said.

Steaming, she forced Tommy into a goodbye kiss that he complained he was too old for and gave Conor five utterly contradictory instructions about snacks, bedtime and tooth-brushing.

"Have a good time," Tommy said.

"Hold out for five carats," Conor said.

"Get a real job," Clarissa countered and slipped out the door just as the buzzer shrilly rang again.

AT MIDNIGHT, on the elevator coming back up to the apartment, Clarissa slipped her heels off her tired feet and looked at the bracelet on her hand.

Diamonds are very heavy—at least they felt very heavy to Clarissa just then. Maybe she'd get used to it, the feel of a large weight slipping up and down her wrist with her every move. Like a handcuff, she thought—and then immediately shoved down her misgivings.

She wanted to get used to diamonds, didn't she?

It was a beautiful bracelet, thirty-two diamonds, each of them larger than any of the engagement rings her Bridgeport friends got when they married. Fred had presented it to her in the limousine on the way to dinner.

Stunned, she had numbly watched him pull the bracelet from its crocodile leather box with a world-renowned jeweler's name stitched on its lid.

"Just a little something to say how much I've enjoyed this visit to Chicago," he said. "Since my wife died, I haven't liked business trips so much. She used to come with me and make any city seem fun. After she died, I never thought I'd think of Chicago as a fun place again. But you've taken away all the gray and all the clouds—thank you, Clarissa."

Strange to have a man thanking you for the opportunity to put a diamond bracelet on your hand!

How it sparkled, how it seemed to draw light from within itself and fling it against the darkness of the cab! During dinner, listening as attentively as she could to speeches and more speeches, she glanced at the bracelet every few minutes.

Clarissa McShaunessy wearing a diamond bracelet! Imagine that!

Wasn't that the most incredible thing in the world?

The little girl who had never had a home to call her own, who had never worn a dress that hadn't belonged to someone else, who had gone hungry many a day rather than admit that whatever relative she was living with didn't know enough to send her to school with lunch money.

That same little girl had grown up to wear a diamond bracelet on her wrist!

And there'd be more diamond bracelets—and emerald and ruby and sapphire ones—if tonight was any indication.

Boy, if the Bridgeport crowd could see her now!

Best of all, she knew this bracelet meant security. What did they say? Diamonds are forever? Boy, if she and Tommy were flat broke tomorrow, she could sell this bracelet for thousands of dollars.

The elevator stopped at her floor and the uniformed operator pulled the grillwork doors open and bade her a respectful good-night.

Why was she thinking about selling this bracelet?

She was going to marry Fred Tannenbaum.

He had all but proposed tonight, telling her that to-

morrow—his last night in Chicago—he hoped to talk
to her about something very special.

If...no, when they got married, Tommy would want
for nothing and diamond bracelets like these would be
just what Fred had called this one—"little some-
things" that she'd get for Christmas, her birthday,
Valentine's day.

Oh, how very heavy all those diamonds felt!

"Home already?"

She looked up from her ruminations to see Conor
waiting at the doorway with two cups of coffee. He
handed her one as she defiantly lifted her chin and
walked by him. She dropped her evening bag and
heels in the kitchen and then walked through to the
spacious living room.

"Where's Tommy?"

"Went to bed at exactly nine-thirty. Just like you
said, Sergeant."

She smiled at his mocking words.

"Homework?"

"All done."

"Teeth brushed?"

"Of course."

"Snacks?"

"Well...we did go down to the corner to get a sundae," Conor confessed. "You had nothing in the refrigerator."

"I had fruit in the crisper."

He rolled his eyes and Clarissa could just imagine
the wheedling Tommy had done for a sundae. For a
moment, scant though it was, she felt at ease with

Conor. Maybe just because he had turned out to be a better baby-sitter than she'd expected.

Whatever it was, it didn't last.

Because when she was comfortable with him, even for an instant, those feelings returned. The attraction. The desire to touch. To kiss. To...

Wait a minute—she was practically engaged to another man!

Abruptly, she put her coffee cup on the radiator cover. Coffee drops splattered the floor.

"I'll get your money," she said, remembering she had left her bag on the kitchen counter. "Thank you for helping me out this evening."

He grabbed her wrist as she walked by.

"Diamonds? From Fred? How very nice," he said, bringing her wrist up to his face as if to kiss, but only to appraise. "Nice rocks. They've got all the major food groups—cut, clarity, color and carats. Lots and lots of carats. But you still haven't closed the deal. No ring."

She pulled her arm away sharply.

"My relationship with Mr. Tannenbaum is my own affair," she said, striding across the cavernous living room into the kitchen. "Now, thank you again for helping out this evening."

"I've got one question for you," he said, following her. "Where's the furniture?"

Her face went red hot. He had asked the same question earlier. Tommy had answered. What excuse had he come up with? Clarissa racked her brain trying to remember.

"It's...it's in storage."

"Tommy said it's being cleaned."

Clarissa's heart galloped. She wasn't very good at lying, hadn't ever wanted to learn how.

"That's right," she said with as much brazenness as she could muster. "The furniture is being cleaned. And then stored."

"Oh."

Like it made sense. But, of course, it didn't. And the way he looked right through her, she knew he knew it didn't make any sense.

"We just moved," she added limply.

That, at least, was the truth, after all.

"That would explain things," Conor said. "Where'd you move from?"

"Philadelphia," she answered truthfully, thinking of the horrid homeless shelter where Tommy and she had laid their heads before she decided to come home.

"So you must be part of the famous McShaunessy family," Conor said. "Old-line Philadelphia. One of the signers of the Declaration of Independence among your ancestors. Now in plastics, I believe."

"Yes, that's right, plastics," Clarissa said, trembling but determined to keep the advantage. "Our family's in plastics." She didn't add that she meant the plastic glassware they give you if you fill up your tank at the neighborhood gas station, but still…plastics.

The McShaunessy plastics family—that was her and Tommy, all right.

Her heart calmed as she struggled to gain her composure.

Conor turned thoughtful. She thought his questioning of her might be over. But then he raked his eyes over her like an eagle zeroing in on a rabbit.

"Maybe it was shopping centers," he drawled. "Lots of shopping centers."

Clarissa squeezed her eyes shut.

"That's us. The shopping centers and plastics McShaunessys," she said at last, reaching for her bag.

"From Baltimore."

"Philadelphia."

"Baltimore."

"Baltimore and Philadelphia," Clarissa said, remembering that she once spent two weeks during her pregnancy in that city, while her husband was looking for a job. "Now, I figure at five dollars an hour, you got here at seven, I should pay you for the sundae..."

"But the shopping center McShaunessys are from Baltimore."

"And they're my second cousins," Clarissa said dryly. "Now I think I owe you twenty dollars plus the cost of the sundaes."

"I think you don't have it."

"Have what?"

Clarissa felt her heart gallop. There was, actually, a fair possibility that she didn't have twenty dollars in her pocketbook.

"I don't think you have a drop of blue blood in your veins. The Baltimore McShaunessys don't have a Clarissa and there's no McShaunessys in the social register of Philadephia. Plastics or otherwise," Conor said, his voice turning dark. "And the furniture isn't out to be cleaned. You don't have any furniture. It's a front, isn't it? A nice, cozy little scam."

Clarissa reached back to the kitchen counter for support.

"I don't have to justify what I do to you."

"No, you don't. But why don't we agree to the facts? You're poor. Very poor," he added, leaning close to her, his breath hot and accusatory on her throat. "But very motivated. When were you planning on telling him?"

She opened her mouth, knowing he was asking her how long she would let Fred think she was wealthy in her own right.

"I was going to tell Fred everything before I said yes," she said shakily. "If he proposed."

"Sure you weren't going to wait until after the final chords of the wedding march?"

"No, I'd tell him. I'd be honest. But I wanted him, I want any man, to look at me as a serious woman, someone to marry and not just to play around with. A rich man knows you're poor and he thinks of you as something to be toyed with. I wanted him to…to love me, to want to marry me, before he knew what I was."

Conor couldn't know how the confession pained her.

"So you have a plan," he accused. "A calculated plan to jump the class lines and snag yourself a millionaire. And this apartment is just part of it."

Clarissa nodded and her shoulders slumped. "Sounds pretty awful, doesn't it?" she conceded. "I pawned my engagement ring from my first marriage for the security deposit on this apartment."

"That's a pretty major sin," he said. "But probably not enough to get you on any talk shows."

He reached out to touch her cheek. She flinched and he looked away, drained of his harshness. He shook his head.

"I have to admire you, in a cockeyed kind of way. You know what you want." He lifted her wrist so that the ceiling sparkled with the reflected fire of the diamonds. "You know what you want and you're going to get it."

Clarissa felt beaten, but she hadn't gotten as far as she had without reserves of gumption.

"I want security for my son," she said with rising indignation. "A good home. I even want more children. I want them to grow up with all the advantages. I want what every woman wants. And you have absolutely no right to judge me or what I've done."

"You want those things. And a whole lot more. You want it all with a few little trinkets from Tiffany's thrown in."

"You don't understand what I'm about."

"Oh, I do understand," Conor said icily. "You have no idea how much I understand."

He turned away and walked to the front door. She let out a breath she hadn't known she'd been holding. She didn't want him to go like this, hating her. But now, now that he knew this about her, she knew he wouldn't want to stay.

"Wait! Here's your money," Clarissa said, pulling twenty-five dollars from her bag. Thank God, at least she could pay him. Show him that she kept her bargains, was an honorable woman.

But he wouldn't give her that satisfaction.

"Keep it, princess. You can pay me next time."

He paused at the door.

"Just one more question."

"What?"

"Have you slept with him yet—you know, giving him a chance to sample the, uh...?"

Whack!

The slap was quick and unrepentant and caught him square on his left cheek.

"You got a good arm," he said, as he rubbed the tender flesh. "And, in addition to my admiration for your strength, let me extend my apology. I shouldn't have asked."

"You're right," she agreed. "You shouldn't have."

She slammed the door shut and slumped against the oak frame. She looked at the hard-won bracelet. It didn't seem to sparkle quite so much. She pulled it off and put it in the only safe place she could think of— the freezer.

There was a knock on the door.

She regarded it warily, then defiantly opened it.

She was ready—ready to explain to him, ready to tell him why, ready to defend herself.

To defend herself to a man whose opinion mattered.

Even if there was no rational reason why what he thought about her should.

But his face—just a little red around the spot where her hand had connected—was tilted in that masculinely arrogant way. Mocking her. In that way that made it impossible for her to apologize, to explain, to rationalize, to even be all that polite.

"What do you want?"

"I'll be back at seven tomorrow night," he said.

"That's assuming your regular girl can't bring her algebra grade up in the next twenty-four hours."

"Why are you doing this?"

"Because maybe you'll succeed. Maybe you'll be a rich lady, and someday when I'm really down on my luck, you'll give me a helping hand."

She was stung by the image, of her granting some largesse to him. It didn't fit with what she felt about him, didn't fit with the kind of man he seemed to be. Didn't fit the cocky guy he was.

"It's a big night for you," Conor added. "If you're going to get that rock on your left hand, it's going to have to be tomorrow. If you can't come up with anyone else to baby-sit, I might be your only ticket to the life of luxury."

"I'd rather..."

But she didn't finish her sentence.

As he softly closed the door behind him, Clarissa vowed that she would somehow, someway find a baby-sitter—anyone else but him—by the next evening.

If she had only done better in math class when she was younger, she'd tutor Whitney herself.

Chapter Six

"You're going about this the wrong way, buddy," Bill said, taking a long, meditative pull on his beer. He leaned into the bar and pawed at the peanut bowl. "You should resist the urge to tell her. In fact, you should let her think the worst about you. The absolute worst. She should think you haven't had a paying job in months, make it years. And she should think you're flat broke and that you've always been that way. She should think you're a lowlife, a real slug. Then you'll know she loves you just for your sparkling personality and your good looks."

"If I let her think the worst of me, then she won't have me."

"So go ahead and tell her," Bill suggested, amiably changing course. "If you tell her, you'll live happily ever after."

"Then I'll know she's only in it for the money," Conor argued. "And you know I don't want that. Besides, would you want a woman whose feelings ran only that deep?"

Bill sighed. And Conor remembered that his friend had seen all the women who came around when Conor made his first, his second, his third million. The women weren't like the ones around the working-class Bridgeport neighborhood—and the difference wasn't just in how they dressed, the perfume that they wore, or the accents that sounded as though they were right out of public television.

No, the women had one thing in common that a Bridgeport girl would never have: ambitions to change Conor. Change him into their kind of man. Fit him in a suit, hand him a glass of white wine, file the calluses off his hands and scratch the neighborhood gang off his address book. A Bridgeport girl would know it was useless—because Conor wasn't going to change. He wasn't giving up his jeans.

And he wasn't—thank God—giving up his friends.

Bill tried one more time.

"Why don't you tell her and then, after she's all over you, get her out of your system?"

Both men knew what Bill meant.

One time.

Conor shook his head.

"She's not that kind of woman. I have a sneaking suspicion I'd only get myself in deeper. Much deeper. She's the kind of woman a man can't forget, the kind a man can't leave."

"So I'll say it again. Don't tell her."

"Then I can't have her."

Bill ground his teeth in frustration. Conor was so determined when he wanted something. His tenacity accounted for his success in business. But this woman was a different matter.

"What's so important about her?"

"I think it's…maybe it's because she's a redhead," Conor said and he told Bill about the girl he had seen so long ago. But it was hard to put into words the connection that he had felt with her.

Bill shook his head.

"Come to my house on any Sunday for dinner and Katie can introduce you to six of her cousins who are redheads," he said. "Bridgeport is full of redheaded Irish girls. Nice ones. Ones that can cook. Ones that will say their 'I dos' and spend the rest of their lives devoted to making yours better."

"I guess I want that particular redhead," Conor said, realizing the fundamental truth. "The one I saw eighteen years ago."

"Well, that redhead could be anybody. She's all grown up now—she could be married, she could be living in another country, she could have a million kids."

"You're right. I should forget her."

"In the meantime, would you please do something about Clarissa McShaunessy? Because she's driving you nuts."

"Should I tell her who I am?"

"No, buddy, I think you should let her find out for herself. After she's married to some other sucker."

WHITNEY BLOOMER got a C plus on her algebra quiz, but the improvement was not enough for her parents to relent.

Ann Joyce had a science project—the feeding habits of the very same iguanas Conor had once cared for— due the next day.

Gail Duncan had measles.

And Pat Ragowski was going to a concert by a band called Goo Goo Dolls. Clarissa recognized this last piece of information as yet another sign that she really was getting older—she had never heard of Goo Goo Dolls and she didn't understand what Pat had meant when she squealed "they're really rave."

And she wouldn't, just wouldn't, call Hallie. Although she knew that Hallie would come baby-sit in a minute, Hallie would also bring groceries for her, buy her a few new outfits, take Tommy on a shopping spree at a toy store, listen sympathetically to the explanation of why Clarissa wasn't married anymore and in general take care of them.

And, just this once, Clarissa wanted to make it on her own. She wanted to prove she wasn't just a hand-me-down girl who needed help.

Clarissa paced and puzzled and read through the Latin School Directory seven or eight times trying to come up with an alternative baby-sitter before she swallowed her pride and decided to call him.

He had said he would come....

Then she realized that she didn't even know his phone number.

There were five Conor Jameses listed in the Chicago directory. She called each of them and quickly satisfied herself that none was her Conor.

One, according to a voice that identified herself as his wife, was away on business in the Bahamas.

The second was a police officer and his mother said he was on duty.

The third Conor laughed when she suggested baby-sitting and promptly hung up on her.

The fourth Conor had a message machine identifying himself as "personal trainer to the stars."

And the fifth was the Conor James who headed up the James Corporation. The automated operator at the corporate offices announced that messages for him and any other of the James Corporation's six hundred employees could be left by punching the pound key and the three-digit access code of the individual.

She hung up.

As if Conor would be the head of anything, much less a corporation.

Although maybe she should ask Conor if he was related to the man who owned the James Corporation. Because if he was, maybe Conor could get himself a real job.

But then there'd be the matter of keeping that job.

And Clarissa had a sense that the independent Conor James wouldn't do very well with any man or woman as his boss.

Even—no, especially—someone related to him.

She dressed as if she were going to dinner, as if she would have a baby-sitter, carefully choosing a rich green velvet that contrasted sharply with her hair which she blow-dried in loose waves around her shoulders. No jewelry because she meant to wear only Fred's bracelet—and hopefully a diamond on her well-manicured left hand before the night was through.

She dusted her face with translucent powder, wishing the freckles looked a little less prominent. And then dabbed her lips with dark cranberry-colored lipstick and flicked her lashes with jet-black mascara. Finally she brushed a clear topcoat over her nails while she waited and hoped and waited.

But, still, Conor didn't call and she didn't know what to do as the clock ticked a bare hour away from the civilized dinner hour of eight.

She was nearly ready to make her next phone call, canceling her dinner with Fred, when the apartment buzzer went off.

Her first emotion was relief, enormous relief at the thought of Conor James coming to her rescue.

Her next was defensive—how did he know? How did he know just how much she needed him? And how could she let herself be so dependent on him?

She didn't like to need him, didn't like to need anybody. Needing someone had never worked out for her in the past, and it wasn't an emotion she was willing to feel now, especially not for him.

"All right, you can come in," she said with all the reluctance of a truly desperate woman.

"Couldn't come up with a baby-sitter you like?" Conor said slyly.

"No, as a matter-of-fact, I couldn't. But when I do you'd better find a real job."

As he walked by her into the kitchen, he carried with him the undeniably seductive scent of garlic, oregano, tomato sauce and parmesan.

"What's that?" Clarissa asked, pointing to the flat box he carried.

"Pizza!" Tommy shrieked, flying in from the bedroom.

"Oh, wow, pizza," Clarissa murmured, putting a

hand to the second-skin layer of green velvet that covered her stomach. "That looks delicious. What kind is it?"

"None for you," Conor chided, playfully slapping her hand away. "Madam probably will be dining at LaScala this evening. They have very, very private booths that have been the site of so many...merger meetings. Specialty of the house is squid marinated in olive oil and tossed with pine nuts, anchovies and kale."

He had guessed correctly about the location of tonight's date, but when Fred Tannenbaum had told her about LaScala he hadn't mentioned the squid. Or the pine nuts, anchovies and kale.

"Eeeooowww, gross!" Tommy declared. "Squid? Kale? Anchovies? Yuck. I don't even know what pine nuts are, but all of it sounds disgusting!"

"Don't worry, bud." Conor winked. "We're having pepperoni and extra cheese."

"Mom's favorite."

"Mine, too. But too bad for Mom."

He looked archly at Clarissa.

"Just one teensy-weensy bite?" Clarissa begged, her mouth watering.

Eight was too late for dinner and she wondered how society people managed.

Conor wagged his finger at her.

"Uh-uh. No way. You're on an important mission. Wouldn't want to ruin your gown with a little spot of tomato sauce. Wouldn't want you getting something stuck between your teeth. No, no, you go on ahead and dine amongst the crème de la crème."

Clarissa swallowed hard. The pizza was very tempting, a lot more tempting than squid. Marinated with anything. Especially kale. And anchovie paste?

Tommy was right—Eeeooowww!

"I've got one more thing to bring in," Conor said, shutting the pizza box on her hand.

He opened the front door and pulled in...

"Basketball!"

Tommy lunged for the five-foot high basketball stand and net.

"Set it up away from the windows," Conor said and shrugged at Clarissa. "If you're not going to have any furniture, might as well make a basketball court out of the living-room. It's certainly big enough."

Clarissa felt tears of joy well up in her eyes as she watched Tommy set up the hoop and begin dribbling down one side of the living-room.

Why hadn't she thought of it? Something so simple that made him so happy...

"Don't go soft on me," Conor whispered at her ear like a devil advising the tempted. "Tonight, you're a woman with a plan. A calculated plan to snare an engagement ring. No time for getting misty-eyed, no time for getting sentimental. Where's that predatory instinct? You've got to close this deal tonight, baby."

"Mom! Look at me!"

Purposely ignoring Conor's cynical comments, she clapped and yelled as Tommy made several baskets. For an instant, she forgot that she was a glamorous woman ready for a night on the town with another man.

With a man who was virtually her fiancé.

She turned around to face Conor.

"Why did you do this for me?" she asked, the tone of her voice the only admission of her deep gratitude.

"I don't know why. Honestly, I don't...approve. But I guess it's not my right to approve or disapprove."

"No, it's not." Clarissa shivered at her own crisply delivered words.

Then, out of the corner of her eye, she saw her boy make another dunk.

"I'm sorry I haven't appreciated you more," she blurted out, realizing that Conor had probably spent what for him was a lot of money on pizza and a net. She also knew that he was a proud man and wouldn't let her pay him back.

She could be gracious.

That would have to be enough.

"Thank you for everything," she added softly.

Conor took her into his arms, and Clarissa thought she should protest. But it felt so good, so right to have him hold her that she didn't say a word.

"Oh, Clarissa, I can't get you out of my head. You're soft and beautiful and tempting and wonderful, but you've also got to be the coldest, most calculating—"

"I used to be a romantic," she interrupted.

"Yeah?"

"And I got it knocked out of me," she said, pulling out of his arms and holding out her vermilion nails for a chip check.

She would not—absolutely would not!—let him see that he affected her at all.

He stepped back, caught her gaze, and held it.

Oh, how his brilliant blue eyes burned! She felt as utterly exposed as a child...was that pity she saw on his face?

Her eyes narrowed.

That was the one thing she couldn't stand. Pity. She didn't need it, didn't want it, wouldn't accept it.

She had outgrown being a tagalong kid with secondhand clothes depending on reluctant distant relatives for her next meal.

She was wearing a dress designed by Coco Chanel herself—even if it had been made in the sixties and had changed hands many times at vintage stores. She had a job, even if it was only going to last until the regular second grade teacher returned from her maternity leave. And she was practically a millionaire's wife.

Conor had no right, no right at all to think he could pity her.

"I'm being a lot smarter about men," she said. "You'll have to grant me that. Fred is a wonderful man."

"Then you'd better get going, smarty-pants," he said, snapping the kitchen towel at her, utterly unaffected by her righteousness. "Your wonderful millionaire will be here any minute."

He pulled out some plastic plates from the cabinet and divided up the pieces of pizza. She wanted to stay, to linger near him, to enjoy a fun evening with him and her son, to breathe in not just the smell of pizza but the air of hominess.

She would trade any of the millions she didn't even

have for this. If this was real. But it wasn't. She had grown up learning the hard way the distinction between something that looked like home and something that really was.

Fred Tannenbaum could give her the real thing.

Still, she couldn't tear herself away, pausing at the doorway to the living room, breathing in the yeasty tomato smell of pizza, watching with pride as Tommy dribbled down the living-room, scored, and ran the ball back up the hardwood floors.

She felt as though the evening were too long and it hadn't even begun.

She felt what any other person would have recognized immediately as homesickness.

But since she'd never really had a home, she just thought she was tired.

"Here, Mom!"

Tommy made a quick pass-off of the ball.

She reached, but Conor, coming out of the kitchen, intercepted with a broad hand.

"No, sport, not to Mom," he warned good-naturedly. "She's gotta watch her manicure. Besides, if she went down the floor in those heels, she'd break her leg. Get out of here, Clarissa, and don't swipe any pizza on the way out. Millionaire's fiancées don't splatter tomato sauce on their dresses and they sure don't have pizza breath."

He dribbled the ball, danced around Tommy and then—with the subtlest of moves—allowed the boy to steal the ball. Tommy went for the layup and scored.

Much high-fiving and backslapping followed, a virtual testosterone festival.

It was something Tommy needed so badly.

Clarissa leaned against the doorjamb, letting herself love this moment.

Just for a little while.

Maybe she would have liked her basketball on a driveway instead of oak wood floors. Maybe the layup shouldn't be so close to the pretty gilt moulding—a garage would do better.

And the pizza...

Well, pizza was eternal.

Dragging herself away from the domestic scene, she picked up her evening bag, pulled her diamond bracelet from the freezer and headed for the bathroom to put on her makeup. She smiled at a particularly loud outburst from Tommy and the *pound-pound-pound* of the basketball on the floor.

Boy, would the neighbors get an earful tonight!

Dropping her lipstick, she dashed into the living room.

"Wait one minute, guys!"

"What's wrong?" Tommy asked, frozen with pure bafflement written over his face.

"No basketball in the apartment," Clarissa said firmly. "The people downstairs will go ballistic. And they should. If you weren't my kid, this would give me a headache in two minutes flat."

"Oh, don't worry," Conor said, flipping the ball to Tommy. "It's after Labor Day. The Yorks are in Boca Raton. They won't be back 'til after Easter."

She was relieved to hear that, but something about Conor's offhanded delivery of the information troubled her...

The buzzer rang. She panicked, wondering if she looked all right without makeup—but she'd have to. Funny how she'd spent hours getting ready and now she felt so chaotic, so rushed when Fred rang.

But she couldn't keep Fred waiting.

Especially not tonight.

"Bye, Mom, have a good time!"

"You, too. Don't forget to brush your teeth," she said. She wagged her finger at Conor. "Make him go over his spelling test practice words tonight."

"Scout's honor, he'll do it all. But just remember while you're gone us lowlifes will be having all the fun. Pizza, basketball… Simple things in life, really. More comfortable shoes, too. Though the ones you've got on make your legs look real nice."

She pulled self-consciously at the velvet gown's thigh-high slit.

The evening Conor and Tommy had planned was tempting— Fred was a wonderful man but this…this would be fun.

Even if Conor did have a smile that hinted at a bunch of very all-American—but definitely not for children—activities.

"I've got to go," she said uselessly.

Her future, Tommy's future was downstairs.

She paused at the door and somehow regained her senses.

"How did you know who the downstairs neighbors are and whether they live at home during the fall?"

"Would you believe I bought their real estate business and made it possible for them to buy their second home in Florida?"

Oh, how she'd like to wipe that mocking grin from his face!

"No, of course I wouldn't believe it. Try again."

"All right, let's see how you like this one. Here I am, a drifter, I get an odd job with the Yorks to, say, walk their Pekingese dogs. They feel sorry for me because I'm so appealingly handsome and so undeniably down-and-out. Still, I lose this job because I'm sooo irresponsible, maybe I show up too late, and one of the little puppies makes a little mess on their fine Aubusson rug. Would you believe that?"

She smiled wryly. "That I would believe."

He shot her a grimace. "You don't have a lot of faith in me, do you?"

"No, I don't," she said levelly. "But if you do a good job baby-sitting, I shouldn't complain."

The buzzer rang again.

"Mom, don't keep Mr. Tannenbaum waiting!" Tommy warned. "Will you bring him up tonight to meet me?"

Clarissa considered her boy's earnest stare. He was pinning his future—they were pinning their future—on a man he hadn't even met. But whose financial worth, whose personal character, was well-known.

She didn't want to jinx anything, but if things went the way she thought they would tonight, she would be engaged. And her fiancé would know that the apartment they lived in was a front for poverty, that the designer dresses were secondhand, that he had been lured in as neatly as any fish...

Would Fred Tannenbaum pick the hook out of his

mouth and walk out on her when she made that particular confession?

The stakes were high and the risks enormous. But she didn't want Tommy to worry.

"Sure, Tommy, I'll bring him home to meet you," she said, tousling his carrot-colored hair. "And, remember, if you don't like him, the deal—I mean engagement—will be off."

She glanced at Conor, thought she saw kindness flash across his hard features, and then she picked up her sequined bag.

She would make a good wife. Loving. Faithful. Devoted. Committed. She wasn't a career kind of woman, although she deeply admired those who were.

No, she'd give a marriage a different kind of benefit. She'd give stability and warmth and caring. She'd be there. Keeping a home. Making a sanctuary for her family. Those things were worth something, and she'd make sure that Fred never regretted marrying her....

"Don't come back unless you've got the rock," Conor teased, raising his crossed fingers in a good luck salute.

"Oh, I'll have a ring on my finger," she said firmly, drawing herself up on her pumps so that she was nearly, but not quite, as tall as he. "And unfortunately, that means you'll be out of a job."

"COME ON IN, DARLING," Clarissa said, leading him into the dark apartment.

Fred Tannenbaum pulled off his cowboy hat and reached for a hall table to put it on.

A console.

A dainty armoire.

Even a Queen Anne style bench.

Out of the corner of her eye, Clarissa saw him adjust to the fact that there was nothing there.

But she had seen enough of Fred Tannenbaum, entrepeneur, in action to know that he hadn't got to where he was by pointing out other people's shortcomings. Even in the home furnishings department.

He followed her through the darkened hallway to the kitchen and, as she hit the light switch, he threw his hat on the counter.

And leaned his wiry frame against the dishwasher.

"Something to drink?" she asked.

"Sure. What have you got?"

Clarissa opened the refrigerator.

It had been raided, as completely stripped of its contents as if it were a tree in winter.

"Milk," she announced.

"Sounds fine by me."

She pulled two plastic Star Wars glasses from the cabinet and poured.

The "plastics" McShaunessy family indeed!

"To us," Fred said amiably.

"To us," she replied tremulously, touching his glass with hers. Their eyes met over their drinks and she was the first to look away. "I've got to check on Tommy."

She slipped off her heels—grateful for the relief— and padded down the hall, careful to keep her stride small enough so that her gown wouldn't be torn. After all, she intended to sell it back to the consignment store.

At Tommy's bedroom door, her throat caught.

Asleep on the bed, Tommy cuddled his teddy bear—the one that had stood by him through thick and thin. And at the pair's feet, Conor sprawled on the floor, a Busytown book open on his chest. Asleep, he was somehow sweet and innocent and still unbelievably sexy.

Stop it! Clarissa shook her head and flipped off the overhead light. She went back to the kitchen, panicking for a moment when she didn't see Fred.

Her heart stopped, and she thought he might have left—knowing that she wasn't who she had presented herself to be.

But he stood at the balcony, the lights of the city spread out in front of him like treasures on a jeweler's counter.

"Clarissa," he called softly. "Come here, beautiful woman, I want to talk about something very important."

"What is it, Fred?" she asked numbly, somehow feeling her future throbbing on her palm.

"I want to talk marriage."

Clarissa felt something welling within her, some impulse that shouted "No!" but she quelled it, thinking of her boy, thinking of the future, thinking of all she could offer him.

She felt her palms burn and she plastered a smile on her face.

"Why, darling, this is all very sudden," she said, with a pleasure she didn't feel.

Fred drew her into his arms.

"What I'm going to do isn't very sudden and you're

probably not going to be calling me darling afterward,'' he said grimly.

"Why not?"

"Clarissa, I'm about to do something noble and unselfish and I don't have too much experience at either of those two things. So I'll say what I have to say and keep it brief. Clarissa, I adore you.''

"Fred, that's wonderful. I—"

"And I'm not going to marry you.''

"Why not?"

Chapter Seven

"What?" Clarissa asked hollowly, feeling as if the floor were sliding out from under her. "You're not going to ask me to marry you?"

"No, Clarissa, I'm not going to ask you to marry me," Fred repeated. "I can't."

"Why...why not?"

"Oh, I could happily marry you, if I was selfish enough. I could marry you in a minute. You don't know how glad I'd be to do it. You'd make a wonderful wife and I think I've fallen head over heels in love with you."

"I would, you know."

"Would what? Oh, I know. A wonderful wife. Yes, you'd make a home for me, you'd put up with all my faults, you'd civilize my little chunk of Oklahoma. You'd even make my friends and partners feel at home—just like you did tonight."

"Is it...because I have a son?"

"Not at all. I haven't met Tommy, but I know it would make me a new man to have the chance to raise another son. No, Clarissa, there's no downside for me. No failing on your part, no obstacle you've created.

Marriage to you would be the best thing that could happen to me."

Clarissa looked down at her hands, feeling as if her future were running through her fingers like so much sand.

If Sabrina was right and her life had only two possible paths... She resisted the urge to stare at her palm, to study it. She lifted her chin and faced the challenge head-on.

"Fred, you've given me all the reasons why it would be a great idea to get married," she said earnestly. "So let's do it. It would be a wonderful thing."

Fred slowly shook his head.

"It wouldn't be fair to you."

"That's your reason?"

"That's my reason."

"I can take care of myself," Clarissa said proudly. "I can decide what's fair and unfair to me."

"I love that tilt of your chin when you're trying to be brave," Fred said with bittersweet longing. "Clarissa, I would gladly be your husband, but it wouldn't be right. Just think of this—when I'm sixty, you'll be..."

"Fifty?" she guessed, shaving off just a few years from her calculation of his age.

Fred chuckled.

"You're either a very tactful woman or the public relations department at my company has been doing an even better job than I thought."

"Well, age isn't everything," Clarissa protested. "Common goals and aspirations make a marriage.

Shared values and mutual respect. We have all those things, Fred, and we can grow into so much more.''

He sadly shook his head.

''Those are very dry ingredients for a marriage. You need passion, Clarissa, undeniable passion to make a lasting union. Darling, you don't have that passion for me.''

''I do,'' she said, but she wasn't a very good liar. ''I mean, I could learn.''

''No, it wouldn't be fair to you. Someday there will be a man who will make your heart beat faster, who will make you tremble with excitement, who will kiss you and make you want more. You should be with that man.''

''Is that a recommendation?'' she murmured sourly, thinking of the sleeping sex god in the next room.

Before she met Conor, she could have argued that she wasn't the kind of woman who could ever be ruled by passion, that the so-called ''dry'' ingredients of marriage were the only ones she wanted.

With Conor in the picture, that was a tough argument to make.

Only she couldn't let Fred walk out that door—especially when the one thing standing in the way of their marriage was his concern for her well-being.

''Fred, we'd be building on respect and admiration and commitment. If passion's important to you, I could learn passion. Marriages grow and change. Ours could, too.''

''We could be married a hundred years and it wouldn't make a difference—''

"But that means it isn't an age problem. How old you are doesn't matter."

"It is an age problem and it isn't. It wouldn't be in a perfect world, but in reality my wants and needs have changed with age—as they should. And you need a husband, a young virile husband, whose passions will match your own through the years. You won't always think you can live without love, Clarissa."

"I could learn anything."

"You won't have to learn—it will happen to you soon enough," Fred said dryly. "But, please, Clarissa, don't skip over stages of life and don't plan the stages of your life for comfort."

"What's that supposed to mean?"

He looked around the empty room.

"The furniture's out for cleaning?" he asked archly.

She started to nod and then suddenly realized he'd heard it before. Not from her. From another woman. Maybe more than one. She felt her shoulders slump in defeat.

"It's a front, wasn't it?" Fred gently inquired. "You're no debutante. Your family isn't in the social register, is it? You're not one of the Baltimore Mc-Shaunessys."

"No, I'm not high society," Clarissa admitted. "I'm just an ordinary south side Irish girl. Bridgeport neighborhood."

"Ordinary? One word I would never use to describe you is *ordinary*. But why this?" He asked, shrugging at the living room with its solitary basketball hoop.

"Why did you work so desperately at making yourself into something you're not?"

"I wanted you to take me seriously. To not think of me as just mistress material."

"And instead, to think of you as wife material?"

She nodded.

"I have to admit you acted wisely. A lot of wealthy men do act a bit predatory toward women from poorer backgrounds."

"But not you?"

"Not me. Clarissa, let me tell you some wisdom that comes from a few more decades and many more dollars," Fred said, taking her face into his hands. "Don't think wealth is going to protect you from anything that matters. Don't think wealth is the only thing that will make you fearless and worthy of respect. You might have been a kid who was bounced around a little, who faced life's heartaches a little younger than most—but you still have to take chances on life. On love. A millionaire's money can't protect you, a nice address doesn't make a very good shield."

Clarissa mutely nodded.

"Face the fear head-on," Fred counseled. "And don't worry about Tommy. You've already given him a foundation of love that will keep him strong. I look forward to someday meeting him—maybe it'll happen when I get an invitation to your wedding. Your wedding to the man you love. With deep and undeniable passion."

He kissed her tenderly on the forehead and went to the kitchen, putting his half-empty Star Wars glass on the counter. He picked up his cowboy hat and turned around for a final salute.

"You've given me a wonderful gift, Clarissa. You've made me smile again. Thank you. And goodbye."

In the half light of the apartment she watched him walk out the door.

SHE DIDN'T MEAN to cry, it just happened.

And she wasn't sure what she was crying for—it wasn't the missed marriage, because she knew herself well enough to recognize the mixed feelings she had about marrying for money.

And it wasn't for Fred—because she genuinely believed him when he said that she had given him something, something as fleeting and as precious as a smile.

And she knew he was right, that marriage between them wouldn't work. Or, at least, it wouldn't work if what they wanted from marriage was so very different.

No, maybe she was crying because she was learning how difficult it was to protect herself from life.

As she raised her hand to wipe away her tears, she noticed the twinkling diamonds of Fred's bracelet.

"Wait!" she called.

Racing out of the apartment, she caught him at the elevator door.

"Fred, I can't keep this. It's beautiful, but no. I can't take it."

She unlatched the bracelet and held it out to him.

Fred shook his head.

"I don't think I've ever had a woman return one of these before," he said.

"Take it," she insisted, trying not to notice the elevator operator's frank interest. "It wouldn't be right for me to keep it."

Fred slipped the sparkling coil of gems into his suit jacket pocket.

"You're an honorable woman, Clarissa," he said, and without another word got in the elevator.

The uniformed operator slid the ornate door shut and Fred Tannenbaum was gone.

Clarissa looked down at her palm.

She studied the spot where the wrinkle of her flesh forked in two directions.

Was her future now as absolutely depressing as Sabrina had predicted?

"Honorable woman doesn't have quite the same ring as wife," a sleepy voice said from behind her.

Clarissa whirled around.

"You're making fun of me," she accused.

"I am," Conor confessed. "Sounds like you didn't get the rock. No wedding march for you."

"And not for lack of trying," Clarissa admitted.

"Looks like you have to go to plan B."

"And what's that?" she asked irritably, sweeping by him to the open apartment door.

He grabbed her elbow and drew her close to him.

"Plan B is...me," he whispered huskily.

He kissed her, once lightly and then more deeply, drawing her sensitive lower lip flesh into his mouth. She resisted, pushing ineffectively at his shoulder and then, just as suddenly, surrendering.

Surrendering to every nuance of his tongue, to the rhythmic caress of his lips. His hands didn't restrain her, they didn't need to. Now they moved down the length of her body to the curve of her buttocks. Sultry kisses coiled up to her hair and down to the base of her neck.

This was what Fred Tannenbaum had been talking about, Clarissa conceded in a blinding instant of reason.

Passion, that's what he said.

Undeniable passion.

But hadn't Fred Tannenbaum sense enough to know this passion stuff was crazy? It muddled the thinking, put the body into overdrive, and made rational decision making utterly impossible.

And, in a final moment of clarity, Clarissa McShaunessy knew she couldn't get enough!

"Mmm, you're like fire," Conor murmured at her throat.

Her fingers splayed against his chest, and then, as excitement mounted, she clung to his rock hard chest, responding to his kisses with shuddering desire.

Suddenly, a door slammed.

Clarissa and Conor broke apart, to find themselves confronted with a short gray-haired woman in a full length sable, a Pekingese leashed at her side.

"Well, I never!" The woman sniffed haughtily as she passed them.

"Come along, Beauregard," she said, pushing the elevator button with a gray kid-gloved hand.

The Pekingese stared with bulging eyes at Clarissa and then at Conor and finally danced to his mistress's ankle.

Grateful to be brought back to her senses, Clarissa fled into the apartment, Conor hot on her heels.

"Come back here," he ordered. "I want to finish what I started."

She lifted up the delicate velvet of her skirt so that she wouldn't trip, and then raced to the other side of the kitchen's tiled island.

"No way I'm kissing you again!" she stormed. "Once was enough!"

He followed her right, then left, but she was faster. He leaned across the island and she jumped back, inches out of his grasp.

"What do you mean, once was enough?" he demanded. "Baby, you were hot for me out there and you wouldn't have stopped for a truck."

"But I did stop—for a little old lady and her Pekingese."

Conor faked left and then right, catching her on the rebound. She struggled out of his arms and this time she meant it.

And Conor always understood no.

He was that much of a gentleman.

Instantly, he lifted his hands up in the air and backed off.

"All right, fine! I'm going. I understand. A truck couldn't have gotten you off of me but a little reminder of life in the upper income bracket did the trick."

"You're right. It did. I remembered that I don't want to throw away my chance at a nice life on an irresponsible lowlife."

"Is that what I am?"

"Yes!"

"And you're scared of one kiss, because one kiss is going to ruin your life?"

"Not one kiss. I'm worried about where it was leading."

"Where was it leading?"

"You know exactly where it was leading. You were on the same train, remember?"

He regarded her thoughtfully.

"Oh, I get it now," he said slowly. "One kiss and you'd want to bed me. Once in bed, you'd never want to leave. And then how would you get your millionaire?"

"That's exactly what I'm afraid of."

"Oh, Clarissa, I had you pegged as an ice maiden, but you're really a very passionate woman. Maybe too passionate. Passionate in a very old-fashioned sort of way."

"What are you talking about?" she said with clenched teeth.

"If you make love to a man, you want to marry him. No slipping between the sheets for a little fun for you. You play for keeps."

"What's wrong with that?"

"What's wrong is that you can't make love to any man who's not a millionaire because you'd rather have loving than money. Maybe you're a failure at being a gold digger."

"You're wrong. I'd rather have food on my plate and a roof over my head than your kisses any day. I might not have married Fred Tannenbaum, but he was…'' She bit her lip. ''He was not right for me, anyway.''

''So you're still committed to your plan to marry a millionaire? Some millionaire, any millionaire, an as yet unnamed millionaire?''

''Yes, I am. I am going to marry a millionaire,'' Clarissa said, with more confidence than she felt. She lifted her head high and squared her shoulders. ''I will choose a husband who will be able to provide security and stability for Tommy and me. A millionaire would do nicely.''

''Then kiss me again,'' he challenged with deadly calm.

Clarissa backed away.

''Why should I kiss you?''

''Are you a romantic?''

''No!'' Clarissa said emphatically. ''Not anymore.''

''Do you believe in love at first sight?'' he asked, coming around the kitchen island to put his hands on her hips.

''No!'' she said, slapping his hands away.

''Do you believe in listening to your heart?''

''No, it gets a lot of people into trouble. Especially me.''

She was backed up against the refrigerator, with no-where to go but into his arms. Still, she leaned back, her breasts uplifted perilously at her velvet neckline. Her mouth open but tilted back not quite far enough to be out of his reach—his breath hot and sweet against her neck.

''Baby, if you're such a cynic, my kisses shouldn't have any effect on you,'' he taunted.

"What effect?" she asked, still trying to hold on to her reason.

"This effect."

He kissed her.

She hesitated, arms stiff at her sides, lips prim and tight, eyes narrowed but not closed. She wanted to deny him, wanted to be cool, wanted to prove him wrong.

But the touch of his lips was her undoing. Her body reacted as if it had been trained for his pleasures. Lightning sparks shot through her body, centering in a humming, aching heat between her legs. She closed her eyes against the flood of stars and fireworks, but giving up one sense—of sight—only intensified the powers of others.

No, no, no! Her reason warned. He could spoil all your plans! Ruin your future! Put your life in shambles! Didn't you learn anything from your one experience with men, your one marriage?

But those exasperated warnings were crowded by another explosion of pleasure as Conor's tongue plunged into her mouth, seeking out each dormant nerve ending.

With one hand she pushed him away, while with the other, she grasped his thick hair and demanded more. When he pulled away from her grasp, her body cried out in despair.

"Feel what you do to me?" he demanded, taking her hand and pressing it to his hard, proud manhood. "I don't like gold diggers, I don't like snobs, I don't like what you're doing, and I think you're crazy and calculating and cold."

"If I'm so repugnant, just leave," Clarissa said breathlessly.

"No, baby, you're like a magnet to me. I can't leave. You turn me on like no other woman. I can't get you out of my thoughts. Can't stop the desire. And I bet if I reached in here, I'd find you feel exactly the same way about me." He swept his hand up the slit of her dress, up the burning flesh of her thigh, and...

Clarissa shoved his hand away.

Thirty years of hardship won over five minutes of pleasure.

"I'm not interested," she said abruptly.

He shook his head.

"Oh, Clarissa, I think you're consigning yourself to the worst kind of hell."

"How so?" she asked raggedly, still trying to reclaim her cool.

"Did Fred Tannenbaum kiss you like this?"

"No."

"Well, I'll let you in on a little secret," he said. "You're not going to find another man who's going to. And, baby, you need it. You're like me—made for passion. You use your heart to do your thinking."

"I'm a woman who is using her head to pick a mate," Clarissa corrected, pulling her hand away from his groin.

"Then, how about one more kiss? To last you through those cold, cold decades of love, honor and cherishing a bank account?"

She shook her head, but her body cried out.

Unconsciously responding to him, she rubbed her thigh along the butter soft denim of his leg. Her fingers dug into his shoulders, manicure be damned. Her breasts, nipples raw with excitement, flattened against him.

"Oh, baby, will I ever have a chance with you if I'm not a millionaire?" he murmured against her neck.

"No," Clarissa admitted.

He pulled away from her and regarded her thoughtfully in the half-light cast from within the thousand windows of the city's skyscape.

"What if I told you I was a millionaire?"

"It wouldn't make any difference," she declared.

"It wouldn't?"

"No, because I'd know you were lying."

Conor chuckled.

"What if I brought in my accounting staff?" he suggested.

Clarissa shrugged.

"It's easy enough to put a few friends up to a practical joke."

"All right, what about a bank statement? A credit report? Annual budget projections?"

"You can forge those."

Conor felt his frustration rising.

"What if I took you downtown to my office?"

"At the James Corporation?" Clarissa asked coolly. "Nice try. But the Conor James who owns it is probably a very nice older man who lives in the northern suburbs with his wife, two kids and a flashy red BMW convertible."

"The security guard on duty tonight knows me."

"So he's a friend of yours. One of your friends who has a job. That doesn't get you to first base here."

Conor slammed his hand against the kitchen island.

"Isn't there anything I can do to persuade you that I'm a millionaire?"

"No," she said implacably.

Conor swore under his breath. Bill was right. She was the only woman in Chicago who didn't know who he was.

And it was a blow to discover she wouldn't accept the truth.

As Conor James, president of the James Corporation, he could have virtually any woman he wanted.

Come to think of it, when he was a teen, he had women to love. Even when he didn't have a penny to his name. What did he have then that made up for his lack of prospects? Had he been more fun? Had he spent more time courting his women? Had he noticed their perfume? Flirted better? Spent more time kissing, more time working up to love? Whatever it was, he needed it now.

"It's time for you to go," Clarissa said softly. "I think it's better for both of us if you do."

She was right. It was better for him to go. And to not come back.

"Goodbye, Clarissa, hope you get that millionaire," he said and walked out the door without a look backward.

Clarissa stared at the door a long time.

He was gone and though she hoped he would come back—even if only to argue more—she had a sinking feeling that he wouldn't.

She had been left by two men tonight.

One, who was wealthy, represented her most precious dreams.

The other, who was a rogue, appealed to her most base desires. So long suppressed, she'd forgotten they existed.

She made herself a cup of tea, knowing that she wouldn't sleep.

Clarissa had never liked goodbyes.

Chapter Eight

"What's written on your hand isn't any different than what was there when you first came back to Chicago," Sabrina told her, shaking her head. "Your hand hasn't changed. Your fortunes haven't changed. You're going to marry a millionaire. That is—" she leaned forward and squinted at Clarissa "—that is, if you want to."

"And what if I don't marry the millionaire?"

Scowling, Sabrina crossed herself. As if sensing just how terrible Clarissa's life could turn out, Sabrina's pet monkey Gervase hid himself in Sabrina's voluminous coat. Sabrina handed him a few peanuts. Gervase reminded her of Maurice, the monkey Sabrina had owned when Clarissa was younger.

"With no millionaire, your future doesn't look good," she said, pulling Clarissa's fingers back to get a clearer look at her palm. "You're at a crossroads. A very important crossroads—decisions you make now will haunt you or please you for the rest of your life and things done now may never be undone. It is the way it is with all women of your age, but perhaps yours is a more dramatic case than most. Choose wisely, Clarissa. That's all I can tell you. The rest is up to you."

"Sounds ominous."

"It's also a time of great opportunity," Sabrina said philosophically. She reached into her coat and scratched Gervase's head. The monkey responded with chattery dulcet laughter.

"Opportunity," Clarissa repeated, turning to watch Tommy playing at the slide in the empty playground where the two women had met. "That's what I want him to have. Opportunity."

She looked across the street at the vacant storefronts. The September wind flung discarded newspapers and fast-food wrappers against the boarded windows and down into the gutter. The gray clouds reflected the mood of the street. People looked down when they walked by businesses that had once brought jobs and money to the neighborhood.

Lack of opportunity, lack of investment had nearly killed this neighborhood, leaving it a graffiti-splattered abandoned wreck.

This had been her neighborhood. Once vital and bustling, filled with people and shops and traffic.

All that vitality, all that energy, was nearly squeezed out of Bridgeport.

There were some recognizable landmarks, landmarks of Clarissa's life that only emphasized the dire conditions.

On the corner was the apartment house where her Aunt Jeanne once lived. She had kept Clarissa for a year until her husband lost his job and the extra mouth to feed strained a fragile budget. The building was an abandoned shell now, its windows busted, its brick facade crumbling.

On the next block was the bungalow where Aunt Karen had lived. She housed Clarissa next, but drinking took its toll and Karen was sent to a state hospital and never returned. The little home had been demolished, but nothing new built in its place.

Two blocks down was where Uncle Marty lived until he was sent to a nursing home. Clarissa had tried to be a help, but a nine-year-old can't keep up with the cleaning, cooking and caring for an elderly man. Then there had been a second cousin of her mother—Clarissa couldn't remember exactly which street they lived on—and after that a childhood friend of her father who lived in what was now a liquor store.

This had been her neighborhood, but never really her home.

A home.

That's all she had wanted.

For herself.

And now for Tommy.

A home that wasn't going to be snatched away from them. A home they could rely on. If this neighborhood was close to collapse, her chances for a home didn't look much better.

"Some developer should come here and clean this place up," Clarissa mused. "It's changed so much in the past years."

"Perhaps there will be such a developer," Sabrina said. "A man who understands opportunity, a man who will reach out and grab the chances in life."

"Well, whoever he is, he hasn't discovered this opportunity yet."

"No, he hasn't come yet." Sabrina nodded sagely. "But it is so difficult for a man or woman to recognize diamonds in a piece of rock or gold in a muddy riverbank."

Groaning, Sabrina got up from the bench and dumped the rest of the lunch bag full of birdseed onto the pavement. Pigeons scrambled around her feet, pecking until the cement was clean.

Then, some birds stalked away, while others flew to the windowsills of the nearby apartment houses, and still others proudly spread their wings for show.

Gervase crawled out of his sanctuary to put his arms around Sabrina's neck so that he looked as if he were a collar on her coat.

"I watched you grow up, Clarissa, and I know what you've been through," Sabrina said. "You've had a difficult life, my dear, and there wasn't much you could do about it before. But now you have a chance to take charge of your future. Make it what you want it to be. Because I don't see any second chances on your palm."

Clarissa started to protest that she wasn't going to live her life relying on palm reading. But Sabrina held up her hand to silence the younger woman.

"Life doesn't give too many second chances. And, though you can dismiss my words as the mutterings of a neighborhood eccentric who dabbles in fortune-telling for the amusement of the children, I'm telling you now as a woman who has lived a long, full life—

there aren't many second chances and you've used yours up."

"No second chances?"

"None," Sabrina said firmly.

She picked up her shopping bag and walked away. Before she reached the gates of the park she turned around.

"Your two girlfriends—Hallie and Maggie—have they found their husbands yet?"

Clarissa felt a stab of guilt. She hadn't contacted Maggie or Hallie since the breakup of her marriage. She was sure Hallie would think it strange to move back to Chicago and not see her. It was just so hard to have either woman think of her as a failure.

"No, not yet," she said simply.

"Then there's more work for me to do," Sabrina said. "I mean, more work for them to do in their lives."

Without another word, she walked away.

"Do I follow my heart or my head?" Clarissa called after her.

"Both," Sabrina said cryptically. "Both, of course."

"MADAM, I LET THE deliverymen in," the doorman said as he held the ornate gilt door for Clarissa and Tommy.

"The deliverymen?"

"Yes, your furniture was returned from being cleaned."

Clarissa gulped.

"Cleaned?"

"Yes, madam. Cleaned and stored," he said without a flicker of interest or disbelief. As if Tommy were right and wealthy people simply had their homes cleared out once a year for cleaning. "Oh, and Mr. James stopped by to remind you that the Cancer Association art auction is this evening."

Conor?

Much as he might complicate the search for her millionaire she was glad he hadn't left for good. Because of the instability of her early life, she had never liked people leaving, even the ones who hadn't been all that good to her.

Her ex-husband was possibly the only exception to this sentiment. Relief was the dominant emotion when he had walked out the door.

And then a horrible thought went through her head.

What if the future that Sabrina saw—the one that was so bleak—was a future stuck with Conor? Or maybe worse—a future after Conor had walked out the door on a very brief, but definitely white-hot fling?

Leaving her with a dismal future with no second chances.

She couldn't let that happen.

She shoved down her panic and smiled at the doorman.

"Thanks for keeping the message," she said. "Did Mr. James say whether he would be baby-sitting Tommy this evening?"

"He didn't say."

"Well, thank you again for handling things."

"Certainly, madam."

"Come on, Tommy."

Tommy followed her into the elevator.

"We have furniture that's gotten cleaned?" he whispered urgently. "You mean, all this time we really had furniture that was in storage?"

"No, Tommy," Clarissa said. "But I think we have a guardian angel."

At their apartment, her hands trembled as she struggled with the key. When she opened the door and let Tommy bound in ahead of her, she gasped.

"Oh, wow, Mom!" Tommy shrieked. "We're like real people now!"

"I don't think a lot of people have a place this nice," she ventured cautiously. "Or furniture this wonderful."

"Wouldn't it be great if they did?" Tommy asked. "Hey! I'm going to go look at my room."

As he ran down the hallway, Clarissa looked around the living room.

Tommy was right, it looked like real people lived here.

Admittedly, pretty well-off real people.

It looked like a home.

Funny how a few pieces of furniture made all the difference.

A couch. A pine cabinet that opened to a TV set. A comfortable chair. A coffee table. And in the dining room, a table with six matching chairs. Nothing too ostentatious, nothing that would have Robin Leach interviewing her for the "Lifestyles of the Rich and Famous."

And yet, everything exactly as she would like to have in her very own home. The one she had been carrying around in her head for years. Exactly like the pictures she had cut out of magazines for years, carrying the clippings around in a little file folder in case someday she ever really did get her own house.

She picked up the plain white envelope on the dining room table.

Dear Clarissa,

I know that you won't accept jewelry from an ex-suitor, but I hope that you can accept furniture back from cleaning and storage. Call it a gift from one friend to another. Good luck finding the love you so deserve and thank you for helping me learn to smile again.

> With fondest wishes,
> Fred

"I have a bed! I have a bed! I have a bed!" Tommy screamed, racing back through the kitchen. "I have a bed with a headboard that's a real basketball backboard. I can throw baskets in bed. Bed-bed-bed-basketball!"

He mugged and strutted through the living room.

"Sounds wonderful," Clarissa said. "I'll come look in a minute."

"Can we keep it?"

She looked down at the letter.

One friend to another.

She sighed, thinking of Fred Tannenbaum. Maybe she really had found a true friend. He was a wonderful man, even if he wasn't a husband.

"Yes, Tommy, I think we can," she said, folding the letter back into its envelope.

Tommy opened the pine armoire in the corner of the living room, switched on the television to a basketball game and flopped down on the couch.

He looked right at home.

"Don't put your feet on the furniture," she admonished and then pinched herself.

It was like a dream!

She was a real mom with a real son with a real home—and even nagging her kid was a pleasure.

Clarissa wandered through the other rooms of the apartment. Tommy's bedroom was furnished exactly how a boy his age would want.

Her own bedroom had simple but tasteful white wicker furniture—with a handstitched quilt that could have been made by Clarissa's grandmother, if Clarissa's grandmother made quilts. A wicker desk and chair stood in the corner. And there was even a wicker planter with a lush Boston fern, with a note from the florist outlining the fern's complicated schedule of watering, misting and fertilizing. Clarissa was sure the plant would, under her care, be dead in a week. But, until then, it sure looked beautiful.

"Mom, can I have some popcorn?" Tommy yelled from the living room.

"Okay," she said.

Everything looked like home.

Home had a very special feel—the sound of Tommy cheering his team, the smell of popcorn in the microwave, the feel of the soft, plush rug on the living room floor.

"Who's playing?" she asked, as she set the popcorn bowl on the coffee table and issued a warning. "Don't get any on the floor or you have to clean it up."

Tommy reached for a monster-size handful.

"Suns versus the Bulls. Bulls winning, of course."

That, of course, meant nothing to Clarissa. But she snuggled next to Tommy who promptly put his stockinged feet on her lap.

"DOES THIS MEAN you're not going to the auction?" Conor asked when he arrived at seven to find Clarissa still in jeans and smelling not of fine perfume, but of popcorn with butter.

Not that he objected.

She had a way of making a pair of jeans look as sexy as a G-string. And the popcorn scent gave her a decidedly domestic air.

But, more importantly, maybe she had given up. In the cold walk after leaving her apartment, he had realized that she had suffered a major blow with Fred not fitting into her plan.

Maybe the shock would wear off, and with it, her crazy ideas about men and money. He had left the message reminding her of the auction just as a way of getting his foot back in the door, but he fully intended on stepping back out if she hadn't changed.

"No, I'm going," she said firmly. "I just forgot the time. The Suns were playing the Bulls. They went into overtime."

She let the front door swing shut and headed for the bedroom.

"I didn't know you were into basketball," Conor

said, following her though his heartbeat drummed "get out, get out, get out."

"I'm not into basketball. I'm into being with my son."

"So stay home tonight."

"You don't know how much I'd love to," Clarissa said, reaching into her bedroom closet for a jade green crepe de chine shift. "But I have work to do."

Conor groaned.

"You're talking about that stupid plan."

"It's not stupid," Clarissa protested. "I'm a marrying kind of woman. My happiness will come from being a wife and mother."

"So why don't you marry whomever you fall in love with? Let it be a natural occurrence, not this campaign worthy of a five-star general."

"But why shouldn't I marry a man who is wealthy and able to provide security and opportunities for me and my child? And why shouldn't I actively seek that husband? Why leave it to chance? If you leave things to chance, you never know how things will turn out."

Conor sat down on the bed.

"Clarissa, you're acting like a cynic and..." he looked around. "Hey, did you get some furniture?"

"Of course I got furniture," Clarissa said. "Typical male, you walked right by two rooms packed with furniture and didn't notice a thing. Tommy's gone to his room and he's going to do his homework on a real desk."

They both heard the unmistakable sounds of dribble, shoot and cheer.

"At least that's what he was supposed to be doing

after the game," Clarissa added. "He's now got a headboard with a net on it."

"And where did all this come from?"

"Fred Tannenbaum."

He cocked an eyebrow.

"It's none of your business," Clarissa chided, throwing a pair of stockings on the bed. "You're the baby-sitter, remember?"

He picked up the sheer stockings and an image flashed in his mind, of his hand on the inside of her thigh. Pushing the silk stocking down and away, like opening a present and finding her creamy feminine core.

Groaning, he threw the stockings on the floor.

This was crazy, he thought. He shouldn't have come back. He had walked around the city all night—ostensibly making security checks on all his properties—and he had told himself a hundred times that he should stay as far away from her as the size of the planet allowed.

He even spent the morning going through his black book, looking for a woman to take out to dinner. A good dinner, a few glasses of champagne, a rendezvous at a nice hotel suite. Something he hadn't done in years—and that abstinence was the only way he could explain how he'd managed to get so hooked on Clarissa. He told his secretary to make a reservation at the Pump Room and he promised himself he would find a woman in his book who would make Clarissa a distant memory.

But none of the names that would have excited him

two weeks ago even prompted enough energy to pick up the phone.

Damn her, he had thought, damn her for making him want her so much!

"Did you say something?" Clarissa asked, popping her head out of the closet.

He looked at her hands. She held white lace panties and a matching bra.

He looked up guiltily, but with enough smoky appraisal that when their eyes met she blushed from the top of her forehead to the neckline of her T-shirt.

"Get out of here," she ordered. "I have to get dressed. Cocktails started ten minutes ago."

Conor swallowed. He felt himself grow hard just watching her bending over, hands reaching to the furthest corners of the closet. Her bottom round and firm, her hair falling in a flame red puddle on the floor.

If she was naked, she would be an offering to him.

Clothed, she was a woman looking for a pair of shoes.

But what a woman.

If only he could persuade her that he was a millionaire.

She'd be all over him.

All he had to do was just lay his cards, his bank statement, on the table.

Be utterly truthful and have all the evidence to back him up. It might take ten accountants, certified copies of his bank statement and the head of the Federal Reserve.

But he could tell the truth.

He wouldn't even have to fudge a few million here or there.

He could have her. He could have every inch of her body. His to touch, to caress, to kiss, to take...

Okay, so maybe he couldn't exactly make love to her right here, right now, with Tommy playing basketball in the next room. But with six hundred employees in the James Corporation, he was sure somebody would be willing to baby-sit for overtime pay for one night.

And what a night it would be.

It was as if she were for sale.

And she was the one who had put herself on the market.

And he was one of the very few men who could afford her.

He lay back on the bed, confident and proud, wondering when and how he could unload the truth of his financial worth onto her, what proof she would require.

"Would you sleep with a man for a million dollars?" he asked, with seeming casualness.

She stuck her head out of the closet, holding up one pale green silk pump.

"If he was going to marry me and I thought I could love him, yes," she said, and returned to her search.

Conor winced.

There was that word again.

The *M* word.

Clarissa wasn't a high-priced call girl he could pay off with a check. She wasn't an adventurer he could dismiss with a nice present from Tiffany's. She wasn't a real gold digger or treasure seeker.

No, Clarissa played for keeps.

Coolly and pragmatically.

Conor had never given marriage much thought, but when he had, he had decided it wasn't for him. He just couldn't imagine loving any of the women he had met so much that he would promise his life to her.

And promising his life to Clarissa sounded downright foolish—if all she wanted was a bank account to warm her bed at night.

Still, maybe there were other ways of getting what he wanted.

He took out his wallet, peeling a hundred dollar bill from a thick stack.

He got down on the floor next to her.

"Would you kiss me again for a hundred?" he asked.

She stuck her head out of the closet, nearly banging into him. She looked at the bill he held up.

She recoiled.

"That's yours?"

"Yeah."

"Did you rob somebody?" she demanded, menacingly shoving the heel of her shoe into his face.

"No!" Conor declared. "I earned it."

"Well, then, you shouldn't give your money to me," Clarissa said matter-of-factly. She turned her attention back to deciding on shoes to match her dress. "Get yourself a place to stay, a nice meal, and a new pair of pants so you can go on job interviews."

Conor bit back an angry oath.

"Just answer the question, Clarissa. Would you kiss me for a hundred?"

"No."

"Two hundred?"

"No."

"A million?"

"No!"

She backed away from him, but there was no place to go except further into the closet and he took advantage of every inch. He was on top of her, holding himself over her. His manhood pressed against her thighs. His mouth was nearly on hers.

He could take her, of course, but he never wanted a woman that way. He wanted her to want him. And he had a suspicion that, as much as she protested, she wanted him.

Against her cockeyed, crazy idea of better judgment, of course.

"Kiss me, Clarissa, do it because you want it as much as I do. Do it without thinking about whether I'm financially worthy of you. Do it just this one time for free. I promise I'll never ask you again."

"No, I won't," she said, and turned her face away from him. "If I kiss you again, I might—just might—fall in love with you, and then, dammit, I'll want to marry you. So I'm not going to take that chance."

"Would you marry me?" he asked, and instantly, he wondered what insanity had overtaken him.

He had just asked a woman to marry him!

He had to be out of his mind!

Worse, he had just asked Clarissa McShaunessy to marry him!

Of all the women on earth!

He had never said those words to a woman. Would never say those words to a woman, particularly a woman whose interests in men was limited to the financial.

On the other hand, no woman had ever inflamed him so.

"No, I wouldn't marry you," she said. "I've already got one dependent listed on my tax return. I don't need two."

He wasn't sure whether he felt pure relief or simple frustration or damnable offense. But he was just sure enough of himself that he wasn't going to let her see that she riled him so.

"That's good," he said smoothly. "Because I don't want to marry you, Clarissa. I have a feeling you'd drive me right up the wall if I did. I was just looking for some fun. Remember fun? That's what people do when they don't have a plan. We could have some of that. You and me. Right over there. On the bed."

Conor felt a sharp pain on the side of his head, right above his ear.

As he slumped forward, exclaiming more in shock than hurt, she wiggled out from under him.

From the corner of his eye, he could see her rapid-fire movement.

She grabbed the underwear, stockings and dress from the bed. She disappeared. He heard the bathroom door slam shut. The lush fern in the corner of the bedroom shook from the impact.

He looked at the weapon she had used on him, lying inert on its side.

"So that's where the other shoe was," he muttered.

Chapter Nine

Monday—the Yacht Club Venetian Night Party. Wore the navy blue nautical dress with matching spectator pumps. Danced with a commodities trader. Later, he confided he had declared bankruptcy two weeks before.

Tuesday—the Art Institute private viewing of the Monet exhibit. Wore the red jersey with the hem taken up. Met a cardiologist. Very nice except he does talk about his work a little too graphically. Maybe he'll call.

Wednesday—dinner and speech on the future of the stock market at the Union League Club. Wore white-and-black houndstooth suit. Sat next to a woman whose son trades bond futures. Possible prospect?

Thursday—cocktails at the University Club to honor the mayor. Black jersey with a new cropped sweater. Didn't meet anyone new.

Friday—?

"Mom, Brian's invited me over for a sleep-over," Tommy said. "Can I go?"

Clarissa looked up from her desk and smiled at the two boys who fidgeted in front of her. Ever since they'd gotten furniture, Tommy had started inviting friends over. She'd have to include that fact in the thank-you note she was penning to Fred.

That was the absolute best part about having furniture—the chance to see Tommy's buddies, even if they did leave a mess everywhere they went.

"Where does Brian live?" she asked.

"In the building across the street," Brian spoke up, coming out from behind Tommy. "You can call my mom if you want, but she said it was okay."

"All right, I will call her. But first I've got to finish this note and find out where I'm supposed to be this evening."

"Yiippeee!" Tommy cried. "Brian, I'll go get my sleeping bag. You won't believe this, but I used to actually live in it."

"Cool," Brian said admiringly.

As the boys ran off, Clarissa heard Brian ask Tommy if his mom always dressed like that.

Clarissa looked heavenward.

Dressing "like that" was a full-time occupation in itself.

Tonight she wore a sea blue chiffon dress that would go with a pair of teal green heels she already owned. Pablo Cassini—in whom she had confided when her checking account got dangerously low—had fixed her hair and makeup for free, calling it good advertising. He had even loaned her the cubic zirconia earrings that now sparkled on her ears like the finest diamonds.

And she had opened a folded magazine advertisement for the latest designer perfume and rubbed it on her wrists and temples. And powdered her freckles. And colored her lips with a toast-colored stain.

She had to admit—she was all glitz and glamour.

Trouble was, she couldn't remember where she was supposed to go.

What party she was supposed to crash. What event she was supposed to attend. Where she was supposed to find that millionaire of her future. Where she would go, she had to be honest with herself, for her evening manhunt.

She rifled through the newspaper clippings, Post-it notes, and engraved invitations on her desk. Fred Tannenbaum had made her work easier—getting her name put on every A list in Chicago's concentric circles of business society, arts society, financial society and just plain society society.

Some nights she was actually invited to the parties she went to! She'd have to mention her gratitude in her note to him.

Still, she couldn't find tonight's event and her day at Latin had been hectic enough that she hadn't had time earlier to figure out where she was supposed to be.

Or rather, where the millionaires would be tonight.

Was it the Museum of Science and Industry fundraiser? She wondered, tearing apart the engraved invitation's envelope.

No, that was next week.

Or maybe the reception for the new director of the Heart Association? She had written the date on a Post-it note. But where was that note?

No, come to think of it, she had already been to that

reception. She cringed as she remembered the stockbroker she had met—he had been very ardent, a real possibility, until she mentioned at dinner on Friday that she had a seven-year-old son. They had parted on good terms.

After all, Clarissa thought wryly, they had something fundamental in common: he wouldn't date women with children and she wouldn't date men who wouldn't date women with children.

She continued to leaf through her mail and then her eye was caught by a plain white envelope which heralded Urgent and Confidential. Opening it, she stared at the sharp, nasty language for several long minutes—heart throbbing, throat clogged with dread.

Another letter demanding repayment.

Her ex-husband might have run off with a dancer, but while he and Clarissa were still man and wife, he had amassed a whopping credit card bill, rent and back taxes debt. And Clarissa had been warned by her divorce lawyer that she would be held equally responsible for those debts, even for things she had taken no steps to create. If the creditors thought they could get their money from her, they'd do it. Especially if there was no chance of getting it from her ex-husband.

She wanted to pay back every penny, if only to have the last bonds of marriage broken. Besides, the creditors were tenacious and she worried that an unpaid debt could affect her and Tommy at some future time.

But the amounts involved were staggering.

And though she knew she would pay off the debt—regardless of whether she was married to a millionaire or single for the rest of her life—the letter served only to remind her yet again of how a woman with poor judgment in choosing a husband could be haunted by her choice for the rest of her life.

Her resolve deepened.

She laid the letter out in front of her and took a deep breath. She'd have to do something about this. And soon, judging from the way the ink on the page fairly shrieked.

"Mom, I'm ready to go."

Tommy and Brian stood together in the bedroom doorway. Tommy held his sleeping bag and a stuffed backpack. Brian stared at her, wide-eyed and open-mouthed.

"Brian, I really do wear jeans most of the time," she explained.

"You look like a princess," he said.

She took his phone number and called his mom to make sure that it was all right for Tommy to go. Then Clarissa sent them on their way—with a good-night kiss to Tommy—that received an "Aw, Mom"—and a promise to Brian that she'd be wearing normal clothes the next time he saw her.

Her heart swelled as she stood at the bedroom window watching the doorman from her building escort the boys to the care of the doorman from the building across the street.

Tommy was happy, truly happy. She wished it could always be like this.

She pushed aside all her money troubles, man troubles, all her worries and concerns. As long as Tommy was happy, she could be happy.

Twenty minutes later, while she was sweeping popcorn from in front of the television set, there was a knock on the front door. Before she could consider the possibilities, she opened the door.

Conor slouched against the doorjamb, and he looked her up and down in a way that made her feel as if she were stark naked.

And yet, there was faint amusement curling his lip.

"I think you've got this Cinderella thing all wrong," he said laconically. "You're supposed to sweep up wearing the rags—and when you put on the ball gown, you put the broom away. Got it?"

She looked down at the broom and the dustpan full of popcorn kernels.

"Cinderella didn't have a seven-year-old."

"That was in the sequel," Conor said, brushing past her into the hallway. He left the faint signature smell of lime and musk in his wake. That smell awakened a primitive, feminine response in her.

Thank God Tommy was around, she thought, because without a chaperon the lure of this man might overcome her better instincts....

Uh-oh.

"Where's Tommy?" Conor asked.

"He's...he's gone on a sleep-over," she confessed. So much for her chaperon. On the other hand, Conor didn't look as if the news filled him with undeniable lust. In fact, he looked a little disappointed.

"That's too bad. I had planned on taking Tommy to the new Batman movie," he said. "He had been looking forward to it, and I promised it as a reward for doing well on this week's spelling test. It was today, wasn't it?"

"Yes," Clarissa said, putting the broom next to the hall console. No way was she going to step any farther into the apartment, giving him the excuse to come in.

But he did come in, sauntering right into the living room and sprawling on the couch as if this was his home and his home was his castle. And it might as well be, since he had baby-sat Tommy nearly every night for the past week.

She had no way of knowing that Conor was only taking his own advice to her—he was having fun. Instead of spending his evenings entertaining clients or planning seductions, he was having a blast with Tommy. Playing ball, watching a movie, eating pizza—even studying for the second grade class's weekly spelling test.

"How did he do?" Conor asked. "On the spelling test?"

Clarissa sat across from him on a dainty, Victorian stool.

"He got a perfect score. He even spelled the challenge words right. I owe you a thanks," Clarissa added. "He said you've been practising every night with him."

"Perfect score," Conor mused, rubbing his jaw. "I'm impressed. He worked hard, kept after me to give him practice tests until I couldn't stand it anymore. How was the math quiz?"

"I didn't know he had a math quiz, too," Clarissa said. She felt suddenly out of touch with her son's day. "Did you two study for that?"

"Every night for the past week. Subtraction facts.

Tommy's very driven to succeed and I admire him. Reminds me a little of myself."

She stared at him, wondering at how he could possibly compare himself to her son. Tommy was a hard worker, applied himself, did his best, had initiative and self-discipline.

Conor...well, Conor was Conor. And, although she had developed a certain amount of affection for him based strictly on how nice he was to her son, she would never think of the two of them as alike.

Conor seemed to be watching her closely. Clarissa bristled. He was teasing her.

"Of course, Tommy will make a success of himself," Conor added. "Not like me."

"I didn't say that."

"You thought it."

"I didn't even... Well, maybe a little."

"My not having a regular job really bothers you. Maybe I should think about looking at the classifieds," he said, drawing out his words. "No, I don't think so."

"It's none of my business," she said snippily.

He smiled. "But it disqualifies me from the Clarissa millionaire marriage sweepstakes."

"Yes, it does."

"Even if I'd make a good dad to your boy."

Uncomfortable under his piercing gaze, she walked to the balcony, looking over the urban landscape, the skyscrapers' lights twinkling in the pause between day and night.

"You can't be a good dad if you can't give him

stability, show him how to live right, be a role model.''

"What about you—I have to be a provider, a stabilizer, a role model for you, too?''

"You have to be someone you're not.''

"You're playing a cold woman, Clarissa, someone you really aren't, either.''

He came up behind her and put his arms around her hips, drawing her back to him.

"You want me, even if it's only because I'm forbidden fruit to a fortune hunter,'' he whispered at her ear, his very breath a caress that sent tingles through her spine. "I want you. This is the way it's supposed to be between a man and a woman. Why do we fight it?''

"We should fight it,'' she moaned.

She turned around, but instead of relinquishing her, he held fast and her arms felt useless and heavy until they were right where he must have wanted them—at his shoulders, feeling the vibrations of his muscles in contraction and release.

"I want you, Clarissa, more than I've wanted any other woman,'' he murmured. "I don't want to want you—but I do. I've never had a woman refuse me. And I've never had a woman lay down conditions like you do.''

She looked up into his eyes, filled with ice blue power and gray steel.

She hoped she would have the willpower to refuse him.

Why, oh why, did she have to feel this way about him?

Why couldn't her heart go *thaddump!* when she talked to one of the bonds traders she met at the art exhibit?

Why couldn't her mouth go all dry when the cardiologist from the Heart Association ball asked her to dance?

Why couldn't her legs tremble when another, more suitable man looked at her?

She looked down at her hand, splayed as it was against his shoulder. Her own hand seemed so tiny and pale, cold now from nerves. But if she turned her hand over to reveal her palm, she would be reminded of all that was at stake.

Her future. Her son's future.

"Would you ever get a job—a real job?" she asked.

"Is that all you worry about?"

"It's not…everything."

"How 'bout if I save us a lot of trouble and say no, I don't want a real job. I'm quite happy doing what I do—on my own terms."

"If that's how you feel, let me be the first woman to say no to you," she said, her voice tremulous.

He relinquished her, but only after a hesitation that made clear that if he wanted to, he could have her. And have her with her complete assent, have her begging for more. All he had to do was take her into his arms and kiss her. Just one more time.

Her thighs trembling, she walked unsteadily into the kitchen and poured herself a glass of soda. The very act of doing something, anything away from him, calmed her nerves. The cool drink nearly quenched her parched mouth.

"So, where are you going tonight?" Conor asked. "Where is your treasure hunt taking you?"

"I'm not sure. My schedule's been so full that I've lost track a little."

"Could it be the champagne and dessert reception for Harkness House?"

That was it!

Clarissa opened her mouth to say yes and then narrowed her eyes.

"How do you know?"

He looked away.

"I just read the society page from today's *Tribune*."

She felt a suspicion, just the mildest twinge. Nothing like the hunches or the lightning bolts of thought that happened to the heroes and heroines of the cozy mysteries she liked to curl up with. No, just a little flicker of "this isn't quite right."

"Why would you read the society pages?" she demanded.

"Just checking for wedding announcements," he said nonchalantly, touching the tip of her nose. "Us baby-sitters don't have a lot of job security."

"That reminds me," she said, her faint sense of suspicion receding. "I should pay you for your time tonight. If I knew what your phone number was, I could have called you and told you that Tommy was going with Brian."

"No, don't pay me," he said, ignoring her pointed hint about phone numbers. "I've got a better idea."

"I don't even want to guess."

"It's not like that," he smiled. "Although whatever

you've got in mind that makes you blush so enchantingly must be something I'd like.''

"Why don't we hear your idea first?'' Clarissa said coolly.

"I was thinking of dinner. Hamburgers. Your favorite. I'm buying.''

"I couldn't do it. It would be like stealing from the homeless. You don't have enough money to take me out.''

"I got paid last night,'' he reminded her. "You even gave me a tip.''

"Just because you cleaned up the kitchen after making pizza. I like to encourage that kind of thing in my employees,'' she teased.

"You'd make a great businesswoman,'' Conor said.

She shook her head.

"Wife. Mother,'' she replied firmly. "That's what I want to be. I admire any woman who can make it in the business world, but I know where my strengths and my happiness are.''

"Wife and mother.''

"Exactly,'' she said. She wagged her finger at him. "And the word *playmate* doesn't fit in anywhere.''

She flipped off her heels and headed to the bedroom to change into jeans before she could see the look of blissful torment on his face.

WIFE.

Mother.

Whenever Conor heard those two words, two very definite, very different pictures came to mind.

Wife—a woman with a ring on her finger and a right to half a man's assets.

Mother—a woman with an apron on and cookies in the oven, a woman with a lot of nurturing for her brood.

Hard to reconcile those two images.

Still, it was even harder to look at Clarissa and think of those two words as applying at all.

Other very politically incorrect words came to mind.

And *playmate* was just the first on the list.

Sex kitten.

Babe.

Goddess.

Conor ground his teeth in frustration.

Why was he here in her kitchen when he could be anywhere in Chicago—welcomed as the financial powerhouse he was, made to feel like a real man?

Under his breath, he rattled off the names of the women who had left messages this very afternoon, each wondering if he'd like to escort them to the Harkness House benefit…and beyond.

And he had been stupid enough to say no to every one of them so he could play baby-sitter for a gold digger too committed to her hunt for a wedding ring to see what he had to offer.

Tommy made it worthwhile, but Tommy was gone.

Clarissa made it torture and of a very sweet kind.

He should go. Call up Ashley, Tiffany, or Lauren. Two weeks ago he would have thought of any of the trio as just delightful. He could buy the best bottle of champagne the nearby Pump Room had to offer for a little after-the-ball fun.

The women weren't bimbos—they came from the finest families. They knew his net worth to the penny and while being seen with him was a little risqué, without that money it would be social suicide. Just not done.

He had no illusions—these women wouldn't see him at all if he still was who he had been, a simple construction worker. But since he owned one of the largest real estate development companies in the city, he was worth placing as an accessory on their arms.

He wondered if they were really any different from Clarissa—she at least was upfront about her requirements.

And he knew Clarissa would be panting for him, too, if she knew what his bank balance was.

But he wanted her to know him as he knew himself: a working class guy who liked to build things, and who only incidentally bought and sold whole city blocks.

A guy who preferred American beer and carryout pizza over champagne and arugula.

Who liked pickup games of basketball, and long, slow, wet kisses.

If she knew him, really knew him, without the incidental money—and still was willing to speak to him—he knew he'd surrender himself to her.

Even if that prospect was damned scary, too.

"Are you dressed yet?" he called.

She appeared at the kitchen door, and he took a breath, feeling as if he were sucking air from a straw.

"You shouldn't bother wearing evening gowns," he said, with more savoir faire than he felt. "Because you'll catch more millionaires in that getup than in any of the fancy frocks I've seen you parading around in."

"It's just a pair of jeans," she said defensively.

Conor shook his head.

"But, baby, it's what's inside that pair of jeans."

"They shrunk in the wash."

"Don't apologize. Those jeans shrunk in all the right places."

"Keep your hands to yourself," Clarissa warned. She saw his fingers draw tantalizingly close to the soft denim and then, at her words, he backed off.

She met his gaze with one that she hoped was strong and steady.

"This is absolutely the last time I'm going out with you," she warned. "It's just hamburgers."

He arched an eyebrow.

"Just hamburgers, huh?"

"Just. I'm not even saying I'll stick around for dessert."

"All right," he said, ushering her to the front door. "Just hamburgers. No dessert."

"And this is absolutely the..."

"I know, I know, I know," he said. "This is absolutely the last time you're going out with me."

Chapter Ten

"You know, Clarissa, you're not millionaire material," Conor said, leaning across the Formica counter at Raymond's Diner, a little dive that boasted burgers, fries and fountain sodas.

Somehow the yuppies of Rush Street had skipped this place. Clarissa and Conor had it all to themselves.

The fact that Raymond's was empty, the fact that it had regular people food was just fine with Clarissa. After a steady evening diet of teensy-weensy cocktail hors d'oeuvres and unidentifiable exotic things covered by gourmet sauces, she was ready for real food and some real peace and quiet.

The plate the waitress had shoved in front of her was piled high with burger, fries and coleslaw. Heaven! And it didn't sound as if Conor was going to bore her with the kind of conversation she had been enduring for the past weeks—where to buy the finest antiques, what luxury car was the best, who to go to for the latest in New Age remedies.

Even better.

"Pass me those pickles, please," she said to Conor.

"Thanks. Why do you say that I'm not millionaire material?"

"You're just not the type."

"If you mean that I'm lower class or that I'm a bimbo or that I'm somehow cheap, you can leave now," Clarissa warned. "Pay the check on your way out."

"I'm not saying any of those things," Conor explained, watching—fascinated, really—as she slathered ketchup and mustard on her already piled-high hamburger and took a first bite. "I'm just saying that you might not be happy being a millionaire. It's not really your personality type."

She chewed thoughtfully, swallowed and daintily tapped her mouth with the paper napkin.

"Great hamburger," she acknowledged. "But I can't imagine how a million dollars is going to make me unhappy or clash with my personality."

"But you're not a millionaire kind of person."

"What does that mean?"

"Clarissa, you're not furs and ball gowns, you're jeans and pocket T-shirts. You're not cocktails at the Ritz and dinner at eight, you're supper at six with the kids. You're not the Côte d'Azur for vacation—you're Disney World. You're not caviar and champagne, you're hamburgers and soda."

"That reminds me, can you order me another one?"

"Sure," he said. He signaled the waitress. "Another Coke for the lady, please."

Clarissa swirled a French fry in a puddle of ketchup.

"All right, so my tastes don't run very rich. What difference does that make? It's easier to learn to like caviar than it is to like soup kitchens.'' She paused, thinking of the party the evening before. ''Maybe caviar isn't a good example.''

''You won't be happy as a millionaire's wife. With or without the caviar. It's not you.''

She shook her head, a lifetime's worth of experience captured in the gesture. She was thinking of the creditor letters piled up on her desk, she was thinking of the homeless shelters she had lived in when things had gotten really bad, she was thinking of the many times she had heard, ''sorry, we're not hiring.''

A millionaire didn't sound so bad.

''I don't care what you think about my personality,'' she said and took another bite of her hamburger so that she wouldn't be tempted to contradict herself. ''And besides, you're flat-out wrong. I think I could very quickly get used to a life of luxury. At least, I could get used to stability and security and living in one place for more than a few months. I guess I just don't care what you think about that.''

''I don't mind if you don't care what I think,'' Conor persisted. ''I'm just worried you're ruining your life with this silly plan to marry a millionaire. The fact is that money doesn't make you anything you aren't already. If you're happy, millions won't make a difference. If you're unhappy, a million isn't going to change that.''

Clarissa swallowed.

''I've never said that money will make me happy,'' she returned. ''I don't believe it will. But given two men of completely equal qualifications and characteristics, why shouldn't I marry the one with money?

Money can give you a lot of security, open doors of opportunity, make a difference in the chances you get.''

"So you're really marrying for Tommy."

"In part."

"And what if you fail in snagging a millionaire?"

"I'm not going to fail," she said, with false but convincing courage. She speared a few more pickles.

"What if you fall in love with someone who doesn't have any money?"

"Are you talking about yourself?"

"Yes. Just as an example."

"Well, get that thought right out of your head," she said sharply. "I'm through with following my heart or getting myself into trouble with men who can't hold down a job, can't remember to come home to their wives, who can't take responsibility for themselves or their families. I've got my future, Tommy's future, to think of. You're looking for a little fling—go look somewhere else. By the way, you're not eating. Can I have your fries?"

"Sure," he said, sliding his plate toward her. "What if I wasn't?"

"What if you weren't what?"

"What if I wasn't just looking for a fling? What if I was looking for a woman to share my life with? What if I wanted a son, a boy like Tommy? What if I told you I love you for the long haul—even if you're a fortune hunter and have the most mercenary ideas about men?"

"I wouldn't be interested," she said primly.

"Oh, Clarissa, you turn so pink when you lie."

She looked at him, down at his hands, so near to her own on the counter. Hers manicured with a pretty luminescent stain. His callused and bruised. Not a good match. But, oh, how she wanted to touch him. Wanted to put her hands into the curve of his, wanted to feel the texture of his flesh against hers.

Conor was the complete opposite of Fred Tannenbaum.

Here was that passion Fred had talked about, but it was packaged with nothing she could live with.

No shared values, no common goals, no mutual respect.

"Are you good for dessert?" she asked coolly.

"Sure," he said.

"Well, then, I'll have the coconut cream pie," she said. "And when I'm done, I'm going to walk right out of here and that'll be absolutely the last time we'll see each other."

"But you need a baby-sitter," Conor reminded her.

"Not anymore," she replied triumphantly. "This afternoon, Whitney Bloomer got an A minus on her algebra midterm. Her parents are pleased. I'm ecstatic."

"I'VE NEVER SEEN a woman eat so much in my whole life," Conor commented, as they walked into the brisk night air.

Rush Street was just starting to fill up with Happy Hour partyers and weekend revelers. Neon lights flashed up and down the strip, and traffic was bumper to angry bumper.

"I forget to eat sometimes," Clarissa explained.

"And then, when I remember again, I'm awfully hungry for about an hour. Then I forget all about food again. You just happened to catch me at a hungry moment."

Even without the full glamour treatment, in just jeans, a sweater and a swipe of raspberry gloss on her lips, Clarissa attracted more than her share of open-mouthed stares, admiring glances and general rubber-necking.

She stepped out into the intersection ahead of him, but he caught her arm, pulling her back to the curb.

"Hey, wait, I thought we'd walk for a while," he said. "You're not supposed to be anywhere for another hour. Don't go on home yet. Maybe we could go window-shopping. You could look for all your wedding presents. For when you catch that millionaire."

She looked up at him and shamed him into letting go of her arm. A group of young suits, out for a good time, swarmed around them and passed. Not before making a few appreciative comments about Clarissa. She didn't acknowledge them.

"Maybe I haven't made myself clear," she said, tossing her hair back. "I told you back at the apartment. This is absolutely…"

"I know, I know. Absolutely the last time you'll go out with me."

"That's right."

"You don't mean it."

"I do."

"You're going to tell me you don't want to see me because I don't have enough bucks?"

"I don't want to see you because you distract me from what I want out of life!"

She looked up at him, challenging him to disagree.

Of course, she was right.

He drove her to absolute distraction. She needed him out of her life—but fast—if she was going to find her millionaire husband.

She turned her hand over and covertly glanced at her palm.

Yep, that break in her flesh where the future either turned very good or very bad was still there.

It nearly glistened in the red glow of the stoplight.

She almost explained the whole crazy story to him right there—showed him the palm, explained about Sabrina. Told him how every night she could feel the line of flesh on her palm in the darkness as she fell asleep. Could hear Sabrina's warning—just repeating what she had already thought about herself so many times—no second chances.

No second chances for Clarissa McShaunessy.

Had to get it right the first time.

But she didn't explain all this.

He'd think she was silly.

It was silly, basing her actions on a fortune-teller's words.

But maybe it made sense if the fortune-teller was Sabrina.

All her life she had been a romantic, had waited for a man to give her a family, had longed with all her soul for the domesticity that some women rejected and others embraced.

If she wanted that life, it was time for her to take action, especially with Tommy depending on her.

"You know what you need, Clarissa McShaunessy?"

"What?"

"To be kissed until you come to your senses."

No, she thought, no to the very core of her being. A kiss would only be disaster.

If he touches me, I won't have the willpower to say no!

He pulled her up to him, touching his mouth to hers with white-hot force.

Around them—traffic snarls and city lights, commuters rushing to their trains, giggling barhoppers, the *clop-clop-clop* of the horse-drawn carriages the tourists rode—all receded until it was just the two of them.

Their lips touching, their hearts pounding, and then their arms, as Clarissa's resistance drained from her, their arms grasped at each other. As if they would never let go. She surrendered to him, fully taking him in, and receiving in return complete…joy.

A feeling that tingled from her toes to her head, exploding her burdens of strain and hardship, and awakening sensations that she hadn't even known were dormant.

Something inside her ached and then burst. A knowledge flooded through her, a truth that she didn't want to hear, but it came through loud and clear.

She loved him.

Oh, dear God, she loved him.

Against all her better judgment, against all the warning signs, against every rational thought. Her heart had destroyed weeks of work her head had wrought.

And yet, she pushed him away, struggling fiercely against what would be her doom.

He seemed dazed by the kiss and she had no doubt that he had been affected as much as she. Did he dread a future with her? Or was he reassured that he could walk away after sating his passion?

She touched her own mouth with her fingers, looking for the pressure point that had been her undoing, searching for the weak spot he had exploited. Her flesh felt bruised and tingly, aching for more even as her better judgment simply shook its head in despair.

"I won't...I won't...I won't..." she repeated, her voice drifting further and further into despair.

"What won't you do, Clarissa?"

She stared up at him, tears of defeat welling in her eyes.

"Oh, why, why do I have to fall for a jerk like you?"

He smiled with a mixture of masculine triumph and boyish delight.

"Clarissa, you tried very hard to fight it but you lost the battle."

He wiped away a tear which had fallen to her cheek.

"Yes, I lost, unfortunately."

"Clarissa, I love it when you're angry at yourself," he said. "Your eyes blaze a wonderful shade of gold."

"It's the streetlights," she said peevishly.

"I don't care what it is, I love it. And I love you."

His words should have made her heart soar. Instead,

she struggled for composure and plotted how tomorrow—at the very latest—she would restrain her heart.

"Don't get so excited," she said.

"What do you mean?"

"I don't want this," she warned, jabbing a finger at his face. "I don't! If you love me, you're just going to have to accept the fact that I...that I..."

"You can't tell me you don't feel the same way."

"I hope it's just the Coke bubbles gone to my head," she said sourly. "And I hope I wake up tomorrow morning and remember that I don't want to love you."

"You look like a woman with a little more loyalty than that."

"I am, that's the problem. I sure hope something tonight makes me change. Maybe you'll belch, maybe you'll get some food caught in your teeth, maybe you'll talk about politics and we'll disagree, maybe you'll hog the bed and take all the pillows."

She caught herself at the last invective.

And so did he.

He leaned down so that his nose was an inch from hers.

"Clarissa, you've just admitted we're going to make love."

"I didn't mean that last part."

"Yes, you did," he said, his smile lazy and slow. "You weren't inviting me over for just a sleep-over. And, darling, if I have to sleep on the floor every night for the rest of my life so that I don't commit the mortal sins of bed hogging and pillow stealing, I'll do it."

"I'm going to come to my senses!"

He shook his head. "Oh, Clarissa, I hope you never do."

He picked her up, carrying her across the intersection as if the curb were Tara's staircase. Some people gawked, but most city dwellers have seen just about everything.

A Rhett Butler swaggering down the walk with his girlfriend in his arms hardly qualified as worth the trouble to notice.

Yet there was something about the sexual energy emanating from Clarissa and Conor—the crowd parted to let them pass, high-pitched conversations paused, a few fingers were pointed in their direction.

"Put me down," Clarissa said, uncomfortable with all the attention though she felt warm and languid in his arms.

She was a feminist, as she should be, and yet relinquishing herself to his strong arms felt good, felt right.

"Oh, no, Clarissa, now that I've got you, I'm not going to be a fool and let you go."

She sensed, however, that if she protested again, he would put her down.

And, now that she had given her heart permission for one night—just one night—of disobedience, she didn't want him to let go.

He walked down Rush, crossing Oak, and then down the quiet residential Astor Street.

"This is insanity." Clarissa ground her teeth as they approached her impeccable, but now uselessly upscale apartment building. "I'm literally throwing away my future. I grew up so poor, so unstable—I must have gotten passed around Bridgeport more frequently than somebody's fruitcake.''

"Whoa, whoa, whoa," Conor exclaimed. "Stop right there. Did you say Bridgeport?''

"Yes."

"I thought you said you were from Philadelphia.''

"That's where my husband dragged us to before he left," Clarissa said, finding it distasteful to even talk about those last rocky months. "Tommy and I stayed for several months after he went. Then I came back here, thinking I'd find my…home.''

She blinked back tears and bit her lip. Hard.

It kept the real pain away.

Conor looked around. If there had been a chair he would have sat in it and cradled his head in his hands. If there had been a table he would have leaned against it and stared at her in raw disbelief. If there had been a couch he would have slumped into it and made her sit beside him and explain everything.

As it was, he had to make do with standing on the street corner with a beautiful redhead in his arms. He looked at her closely. The hair was that shade of burgundy and fire. Darker now than his memory allowed, but still….

"How old did you say you were?" he asked, steel eyes narrowing.

"Thirty."

"Did you ever go to SummerFest?"

"Every year," she said, relaxing a little. "I hated the roller coaster. Loved the fortune-teller Sabrina. Got sick on the cotton candy every year.''

He smiled weakly, thinking he could hear the strains

of "Two Out of Three Ain't Bad" in his head, smell the burgers and onions on the grill, feel Bill at his shoulder, and of course, see her from a distance.

A distance of years, of so much nearly buried memory.

Here was his redhead, his at last.

He felt everything come together, as smoothly and as definitely as the pieces on a jigsaw puzzle. He understood her, understood everything—and it came from a distant memory of how she carried herself, of her shadowed smile, of a connection that he felt because of his own troubles.

He knew he would always look on this moment as when he fell in love. For the first time. When he knew that loving Clarissa would be with him forever. He wouldn't lose it overnight. Wouldn't lose it as he aged. It would always be there. And now he understood that everything he had ever done with any other woman had only been a pale imitation.

It was difficult to put these feelings into words, he realized. He was a man who created with brick and steel and mortar. With buildings. Never words.

"Clarissa, fate has put you in my path," he said, deciding he would explain later the complicated and tangled emotional journey he had taken since he was seventeen. "Maybe you're just going to have to accept that you're going to be mine."

"Just 'til tomorrow?"

"No, this is for forever," he said, and then he remembered that she still thought he was a poor no-account. "You'll have to get a better paying job."

"I guess I would have to if I was stuck with you."

"You'll have to put up with all my faults."

"Yuck," she said mockingly.

"They're not big faults. I don't drink or do drugs, I don't hit women or kids, I don't stay out too late at night, and I don't tell Tommy that most of what he learns in school isn't going to be worth a hill of beans in real life."

"But you don't have a regular job."

He smiled, taunting her, truly enjoying himself.

Clarissa growled in frustration.

"Sorry, Clarissa, I don't have a regular job."

"Do you have a savings account?"

"You mean a passbook kind, the kind in a bank? No, I don't think I do."

"And you don't have a home?"

"No, but I'm eyeing a little place in Bridgeport."

"You probably can't pay for it," Clarissa warned. "Although Bridgeport's looking so down these days, who knows? Maybe it's the only place in Chicago you can afford."

"I'm talking to venture capital people tomorrow."

"I'll bet," Clarissa said grimly. "Stop teasing me."

At her building, the doorman didn't flinch.

"Good evening, Mr. James, Miss McShaunessy," he said, pulling open the gilded door without so much as a flicker of untoward interest.

The elevator operator expressed the same solicitous politeness, devoid of apparent curiosity. He had seen everything.

All the while, Clarissa's mind churned. Never had she felt herself so split in two, as divided as the line on her palm. Her body aching for his touch. Her reason screaming "No!" And her emotions stretched to their breaking point—between exultation and doom, ecstasy and heartache.

He put her down at the apartment door so she could fish her keys out of her back pocket. At least, she thought they were in her back pocket.

"Here, let me help," he said.

From behind her, he put both hands in the front pocket of her jeans, kneading the tender flesh between her hip bones and pubic mound. Her head dropped backward, her back arched, and her buttocks ground back into him.

"Clarissa," he moaned, deep in his throat.

She exhaled, feeling suddenly how right this was. How it was meant to be, even if she had worked so hard for another fate. She couldn't deny her urgency.

Tomorrow, she thought in some deep recess of her mind. She'd have to face the consequences tomorrow.

She felt the creamy texture of her excitement and closed her eyes.

A hallway door slammed.

Clarissa and Conor looked up.

"You people are disgusting!" The sable-coated woman hissed. "Come along, Beauregard, disregard these two. Shut your little eyes."

The woman marched past them, Beauregard the Pekingese prancing at her heels. The elevator operator responded immediately to the woman's call.

Clarissa looked up at Conor.

This was the moment to back out.

This was the moment for indignation.

This was the moment to send him packing.

Instead, she wagged her finger at him.

"Tomorrow morning you're out of here," she said sternly. "This is absolutely—"

"I've got it, Clarissa. You can say it as many times as you want."

"Absolutely the last time I'm going to see you."

Chapter Eleven

She pulled him inside the dark apartment but evaded his ardent embrace.

"The answering machine," she explained, striding to the armoire in the living room where she kept the machine stashed.

"What are you checking for—another date from some stockbroker?" Conor asked, flipping on the switch for the glittering foyer chandelier.

She heard the barely there annoyance.

"No," she explained patiently. "I'm checking for Tommy. Since there's no messages on the machine, it means he's having a good time at his sleep-over. If he left a message asking me to come get him, this little party would be over immediately. Let me warn you right now—if he calls homesick, you're out of here without any questions, before he gets back to this apartment. My weaknesses aren't something I want him to deal with, don't want him to see me in bed with a man."

"Even if it's me?"

"Especially if it's you. Oh, and one other thing."

"Yeah?"

"If the Sultan of East Brunei had left a message saying he wanted to dine with me at the Ritz-Carlton, I might have sent you packing, too."

He caught her teasing tone—still, both of them were uncertain just what would happen if the richest bachelor in the world called.

"Come here, you little vixen," Conor said, taking her arms and pulling her into his embrace. "Do you know how much I don't want to want you?"

"About as much as I don't want to want you?"

He nodded.

"You're a gold digger."

"You're a no-account."

"You're calculating."

"You don't understand the practical mathematics of the world."

"I don't appreciate a woman judging a man solely on the size of his wallet. But I love you all the same."

"I don't like men who haven't grown up, who can't act responsibly."

"Then we're even. We have a lot we don't like about each other"

"I suppose we do."

"Would you love me if I had a job and promised to keep it until they gave me a gold watch and a retirement party?"

"It would make you a little more attractive," Clarissa conceded, suppressing a moan as he kissed her neck. "Would I be more beautiful if I took a vow of poverty?"

"As long as it wasn't a vow that included chastity, I'd be okay with it."

"We're not made for each other."

"I thought you'd say that."

"We'd have to give up everything at the core of us to stay together," she said. "I'd have to give up wanting a better life. You'd have to give up...being irresponsible. But I guess you aren't even meaning this to last past tomorrow morning anyhow."

"I thought you were the one who was hoping I'd hog the pillows or belch loud enough for the neighbors to hear. That way you could throw me out with a clear conscience and no regrets."

"Is this a one-night stand?" she asked, the wobble of her words giving away her fears.

"Only if you want it that way."

"You're probably thinking I'm the kind of woman who would support you. You'd be a fool to walk out on me in the morning when I—"

He covered her mouth with his hand.

"No, Clarissa," he whispered. "Don't question my honor. I'm an old-fashioned guy. A man, not a pet. Let's not ruin tonight by arguing. We have the rest of our lives for that."

He pulled his hand away from her, but she remained silent. Watchful. Wary. Ready for him. But uncertain. Teetering on the edge of disaster. Or bliss.

With his hand cupping the back of her neck, he steadied her head. He kissed her once, twice and again on the base of her throat. Clarissa's eyes squeezed shut in torment. She wanted those kisses...everywhere.

"All right. Why don't we think about tomorrow tomorrow?" she murmured huskily.

He kissed her again.

"When you're gone," she added pointedly.

"You agree we shouldn't talk tonight?"

She jerked her head up and looked at him with eyes narrowed.

"I guess I'm resigned to my fate tonight," she said.

"So am I."

"Why do you look so smug about it?" she asked.

"Because I might still have a few tricks up my sleeve."

"I'll just bet you do."

"No, really, Clarissa, maybe I should just tell you now and get it over with. I haven't told you because I've wanted you to love me as I am and not how I have become."

She put a finger, scorching hot, to his lips.

"Don't talk. Don't tell me anything. Don't make me any promises. Don't tell me some new scheme you have for turning your life around. Men say all kinds of things when they're trying to get a woman into bed. And I'm telling you that you don't have to say a word to get there. Let's just make love and try not to argue too much on the way there."

"You make making love sound like taking that final walk down death row."

"My last hope is that making love once will get it out of my system. Because I fully intend this to be absolutely the last time I see you. If I don't get over you...well, you told me not to say anything to impugn your honor so I won't say anything. But I have a feeling that you're hoping that a single night in bed with me will be enough to last you a lifetime. And I'm hoping the same thing."

Conor recoiled. And immediately had to admit to himself that he had once thought the same thing.

And it was a strategy that had worked—with other women.

Often a nagging desire for some starlet or society girl had been quenched in one night. He always made sure to never promise more and he often sent women on their way with a very extravagant present from Tiffany's and a wry speech on how he wasn't good enough for them.

Now, with Clarissa in his arms, he knew his love for her could only deepen with the consummation of their passion. One taste of her honey-sweet core, and he would be as leashed to her as if by the heaviest cable. She was, after all, taking him as he was—as he was a long time ago. She was taking him as a poor man, as a man of few prospects, as a man with no diamonds or furs or mansions to offer.

But what if she woke up tomorrow and sent him packing?

Ah, yes, he had his final card to play. His own wealth. He'd almost told her many times—the last being about thirty seconds ago—but now he decided it would wait until the morning.

When both of them would be a hell of a lot more rational than they were now. And when he could amass the kind of proof she would require. Accountants and spreadsheets and certified bank statements.

Then, they could live happily ever after.

Tonight, they could take their time.

"Then let's," he unbuttoned the top button of her

blouse, "get down," he undid the second, "to business," he finished, plucking the last button apart.

He pulled off her shirt.

"What?" Clarissa demanded, her defiant chin tilted upward as he stared with amusement at her.

"Is this cotton thing what you're showing to the finest men of this city?"

He fingered the worn cotton bra with its Swiss dot pattern. A tiny gold safety pin held together a tear.

Clarissa crimsoned.

"No one's seen my underwear," she said huffily. "I haven't made love to anyone...yet."

"Well, I knew Fred had been a gentleman, but all the other men you've been wined and dined by—they haven't had even the teensiest little peek?"

"None of them. Not that it's any of your business."

His heart soared at the knowledge—though he couldn't put his finger on why it even mattered to him.

"It's cute," he said, pushing her blouse from her shoulders and unclasping the bra at its back. "I like it. But when you do make love to a millionaire, don't you think you should spring for some of the fancy silk stuff?"

"I'll keep that piece of advice in mind. When the time comes, I'll be prepared."

He came around behind her and ran his hand up her spine, delighted as she shivered. Then he put his hands under her arms and squeezed both firm, ripe breasts. Her head dropped back onto his shoulder.

"Ah, Clarissa," he murmured. "How did you ever expect to capture a millionaire without sleeping with one?"

"With something you'll never have."

"What?"

"Class."

She pushed his hands away but brought them back immediately to her hardened nipples. Conor saw the war within her. The willfulness saying no. The womanliness saying yes.

Unzipping her jeans with one hand, he pushed them down to her ankles with the other. He stood up and looked at her nakedness.

What a goddess.

When she said class, she was absolutely right.

And yet, no ordinary stockbroker or lawyer with a trust fund deserved her.

But did he? He looked down and saw his own callused hands. A blister on his hand from breaking ground on the Bridgeport project—he liked to get down and help his men, looked down on those investors who wore pinstripes and hard hats and couldn't tell a wrench from a crane. But maybe those men were exactly the sort who were made for Clarissa.

Was he good enough for her? Were these hands good enough to touch her flesh?

Conor didn't know the answer to that—but he knew he had to have her. That he loved her. For always.

He circled her, feeling something like a pasha regarding a purchased harem slave, yet deriving so much pleasure from her beauty, a beauty that was for him, for tonight. She was his, to take, to savor.

Then he knew that if Clarissa ever made love to one of her millionaire prospects she would have a selection of Tiffany's finest rings to chose from by morning.

Any man who saw her in her perfection would want her—in the parlance of the wealthy, to own her.

"You shouldn't have bothered with the evening gowns," he whispered. He thought of a most indecent style of auction. "You could have had twenty proposals if you'd just shown them this."

"I was banking on this being a wedding present to give to my very wealthy, very responsible groom. If I had 'showed' anyone this, I'd be a man's mistress, not his wife."

"And now you're giving it to the very poor, very irresponsible Conor James? And you don't even want the Mrs. title that could come with it?"

"Don't make me answer that."

She looked up at him, a strange mixture of meekness and pride on her face. He put his palm on her thigh, near the triangle of pale strawberry-colored hair. He felt her shiver.

And he felt something he had never felt when making love to a woman—he felt responsible not merely for her physical pleasure, but for her feelings. For the woman who was opening her body to him.

Who was opening her heart to him.

So this was what loving a woman meant. Oh, God, he had had no idea how much it transformed a man.

"Now it's your turn, Clarissa," he urged gently.

He drew her hand up to his shirt collar. And helped her with every button, helped her to pull his shirt away, pushed his jeans down and kicked them away. And then he stood, hard and proud, a man.

Ready for her.

She came into his arms in a trembling rush but he

held her away. Even as he wanted to take her right there, right then.

"No, no, Clarrisa, I want you to look at me," he said. "You should know what you're getting."

Her eyes danced with fire and champagne glints. She held his gaze and then, her eyes darted away. First, down to the floor. And then, slowly, so slowly, up his body—until he felt like the love slave and she his master.

"It's for pleasure," he said, as her eyes lingered. "It's every inch for pleasure."

She met his eyes again.

"When you decide to be a responsible adult, I have a couple of career choices to suggest," she said playfully. "And none of them require a college degree."

She walked around behind him and put her arms under his and around to his smooth, muscled chest. He ached as he felt her body behind his, teasing him with tantalizing, seemingly accidental brushes of her breasts, her legs, her stomach.

He looked around the half-lit living room. The couch seemed weird, especially since he associated it with watching the games with Tommy. The armchair was too small, had always made him feel as if he were sitting on furniture from a doll's house. The rug was Aubusson, which if he had been born to wealth he would have considered it sacrilege to even step upon the antique, hand-woven wool much less make love on it—but Conor was thinking more of comfort.

And the long, slow time he intended to spend making love.

He moaned as she kissed the triangle of muscle between his shoulder blades.

"Clarissa, should we maybe find a comfortable place to continue?" he asked, turning around and taking her hands into his. "I want to take my time, I want to feel good. If you pick the chandelier, I think it can't hold both of us. If you pick the dining room table, it'll be mighty uncomfortable after a while…"

"The bedroom," Clarissa whispered.

"Oh, Clarissa, you are at heart a most conventional woman," he teased.

He picked her up, awestruck again at how light, how good, how right she felt in his arms. He carried her to the bedroom, switched on the dim overhead chandelier and laid her on the bed. He flicked back the pale gold lace sheets. Her red hair splashed against the pillows, a sharp contrast to the rich fabric, it blazed burgundy and fire.

"Fred has good taste in sheets," he murmured.

"You sound like you know him."

Conor bit his lip. He had nearly blown his cover.

"No, just through you," he lied. "Now, where was I?"

Clarissa laughed. "I think you were at the part where you were explaining that your body is made for pleasure."

"Oh, yes."

Her laughter was like the playful running water of a pebble-strewn brook, but it caught in her throat as he kissed the baby-fine line of hair between her belly button and her pubic mound. She gasped and he thought he heard her say his name.

Her belly was soft, not as flat and rock-hard as a teen who had never given birth, but it was womanly and gave him pleasure. His kisses moved downward until he inhaled the soft musk scent of her.

"Darlin', you've got to uncross your legs if we're going to have any fun."

"It's just, it's just…they're shaking."

"That's because you're excited. Haven't you ever been…?"

She shook her head, biting her lip. Suddenly, the always confident, mostly self-assured woman was gone. Replaced by the very real, very shy Clarissa.

"I know I act pretty sophisticated. But I never, with my husband, I mean, I never…"

"You never— Never what? How did you ever end up with Tommy?"

She blushed scarlet.

"I don't mean I never did that. I mean, I never…had an orgasm."

Conor took a minute to absorb this. This was one thing he never would have guessed. Clarissa always seemed so sure of herself—certainly she was as sure of her sexuality. Wasn't she?

"Never?" he asked. "How long were you married?"

"Three years."

"Three years? And you never once…?"

"It's not that he didn't try. He did everything…but he said I might be frigid. So, if you make love to me and I don't respond the way you think I should, then you should chalk it up to my being…"

Conor laughed. Hard. He hadn't heard something so

ludicrous in his life. Then he saw how serious she was, about to cry really, and he put a lid on his mirth.

"Clarissa, I have never met a woman who is less frigid. You're the most sexual woman I know. You walk down the street and it's a sexual event."

"But I've never had an orgasm!"

"You're going to tonight."

"How do you know?"

"I just know."

"Is this bragging?"

"It might be. But I'd be willing to bet a million dollars you're going to have an orgasm tonight."

"You don't even have a million dollars," she said with more bravado than he knew she felt. "Otherwise I'd bet you a million that I won't."

"Yeah, but you're such a gold digger..."

"A not very successful one if you're in my bed," she stated.

"True. But as an aspiring gold digger, you'd figure out a way to have me pay you a million for every orgasm you have."

"That sounds like a great bet," she teased. "If you're as good as you think you are and as wealthy as I wish you were, I'd win twice over. But you don't have any money."

He almost said it, right then, but he didn't want to get off the topic, didn't want to get sidetracked from his exploration of her body. Anyway, she'd never believe him, not here, not now.

Besides, this was just a queen-size bed, Conor observed, not large enough to accommodate the sixteen accountants, bankers, investment advisors and lawyers she'd need to persuade her that he was who he was.

"Darling, let's just pretend I have it," he said. "And let's just pretend I'll pay you. And let's just pretend you're not scared to death of me."

She bolted upright.

"I am not scared to death."

"All right, not scared to death. But pretty close."

Their eyes met. The dark interior of her champagne eyes deepened and then paled.

"All right, pretty close to scared to death," she admitted.

She lay back against the pillows, watching wide-eyed as he spread her legs and laid down between them. As he stroked the soft, pale flesh of her thighs with his fingers and then his tongue. As he coaxed them to quiet, to stop their fretful tremors.

And only then did he taste the honey-sweet and silky soft flesh of her womanhood. She moaned from deep within her throat. He felt her whole body tense and then surrender as languidly as the waves of a calmed sea. Her hips moved in rhythm to his tongue's caress, at first following, always following, and then, with more urgency, coming to him and then leading him on. Her fingers twined in his hair.

He felt his own hardness and forced himself to not lose control.

Not yet, not yet, he told himself, straining against the exquisite torture.

But she couldn't discipline her body as well as he, having never needed to develop any talent at stopping sexual response.

She erupted in a sudden, convulsive sob accompanied by a bucking of her hips, and a cry that he heard as a tender sob. He placed his palm against her flesh, feeling the contractions. Again and again. Like concentric circles as a rock thrown on water. And he looked up, to see her face thrown back against the lace pillow.

Oh, how beautiful she looked in ecstasy, mouth parted, eyelashes fluttering against her cheeks, hair tossed back in abandon, a red flush on the base of her throat. And then, he thought he saw tears, but they were gone with a quick flick of her wrist.

He checked his own body responses as she stilled. He forced his heartbeat a little slower, his breathing a little calmer, his muscles to relax just a little bit.

Then she opened her eyes and looked at him.

"Why, oh why, did I have to fall in love with such a wonderful, wonderful, wonderful louse like you?" she asked.

He could control everything about his body except his smile. It was broad and warm.

She loved him. She loved him for what he was, and him being a millionaire would only be a wonderful surprise that he would give her.

He would tell her everything—about the first time he ever saw her, about his battle to feed his abandoned family, about his rise to wealth. Everything about himself. Everything that mattered. Everything that would cement them together and brush away her fears and insecurities.

Later.

For now, he had other things on his mind.

He lifted himself up to her side, wiping the musk smell from his mouth.

"I owe you a million dollars," he said, his hands gently caressing her breasts, teasing the nipples to hardness.

"What are you doing now?"

"Losing a second million, if I'm lucky."

Chapter Twelve

"Another million?"

"Another million," Conor confirmed, wondering how late his personal banker could do wire transfers into Clarissa's checking account. "This time we'll try something a little different."

Without quite understanding what she was doing, Clarissa assumed the pliant position that her ex-husband had unwittingly taught her. The position for sex for the desperate last months, when they had long since given up on the idea that she would be... responsive. When they had both long since given up trying.

"No, no," Conor said, grinding his teeth as he thought of the jerk who had been her husband. How could a man not see the fiery sexuality in Clarissa? How could a man not want to honor and free the woman within? "I'm not...ready, and besides, we're not playing statue tag."

"You are too ready."

"Okay, I admit, I might be ready. Hell, I've been ready since the moment I met you, but you aren't. You need some time to recover."

"I find it incredible enough that I did it once, I don't think I could ever do it again—much less in the very same evening."

She spoke straight from the heart. The physical experience of orgasm had been incredible. Having an orgasm was like exploding every thought, every sensation, every emotion. For a few torturous seconds, she had thought the earth was collapsing from under her—that Chicago, of all places, was having an earthquake. That Lake Michigan had risen from its bed with tidal wave force. That skyscrapers were falling like Lincoln Log construction toys.

But even those disastrous possibilities hadn't made her want to stop.

How her emotions swirled. She was grateful and happy and calm and excited all at the same time and in greater measure than she had ever felt.

And when it was over, what did she feel?

Love. And peace.

More fully and deeply than at any time in her life—with the possible exception of the moment she first saw Tommy.

How was it possible that Conor had opened the lock on her? A lock that had been the one thing that had made her believe, really believe, that a marriage based on the dry values of shared respect and values and security would be enough. With this new knowledge, a knowledge deep inside her body, she knew she couldn't spend the rest of her life vowing to love, honor and cherish a man with whom she couldn't share this.

Oh, how Fred Tannenbaum turned out to be exactly right.

Passion. Undeniable passion.

That's what made a marriage.

And here was the one man who unlocked her body's secret.

Conor James.

And here there was a pause in her calming ecstasy.

Conor was most definitely not the marrying type. Not that she would marry a man like Conor. It would be a disaster if she did. Why did she have to have such lousy judgment in men?

She shoved aside her painful, conflicting thoughts.

This night was too much pleasure to waste a second worrying about the rest of her life.

He slid between her legs and nearly, but not quite, entered her.

"Every inch of me is for you," he said.

And he came into her, slowly and fully, touching the achingly virgin inner spot of her womb.

"Oh," she said simply.

"What does that mean?"

"It means I didn't know."

"You didn't know?"

"No, I sure didn't."

"Didn't know what?"

"That it could feel...this nice."

He groaned.

"Oh, Clarissa, this is just the beginning."

With perfect understanding of her body's pleasure, he paused within her. Waiting. With the patience of a real lover.

And then she felt herself move against him. Grinding, pulling, pulsating, swirling—a seductive dance at its most wanton and base. Her eyes held his, and she watched as they seemed to turn to liquid. She had him completely under her control, guiding his pleasure by her moves. And yet, he had her—because she felt *it* again as he touched her again and again.

There at the core of her.

Her legs spread against the sheets and then, as if they had known all along the secrets that her brain had not, they locked around his back, and he came deeper into her. Her eyes focused on his, looking for the loving reassurance and finding it there.

And then, as the eruption of his passion matched hers, she closed her eyes only to feel his kisses on her lids. She felt like a satisfied wanton as she pulled him farther into her, willing him the same pleasure that he had given her.

"Oh, Clarissa," he whispered and he moved against her and then, after an explosive pause, stilled.

His ragged breath touched her ear.

She smiled. But was glad that in the darkness he couldn't see just how much she had been transformed by his lovemaking.

"That's two million you owe me, Conor James," she said, struggling to regain her self-assured confidence.

"Don't worry, I'll pay," he replied good-naturedly. "And be very happy when I do."

She closed her eyes, spent. Never more relaxed in her life, never more exhausted. She felt so safe, so perfectly at peace. Within seconds of him curling his arms around her, she drifted into a deep, dreamless sleep.

But while she was given a peace that let her rest, Conor was energized by the lovemaking.

"You know what we're going to do first thing in the morning?" Conor whispered into the darkness. "I'm going to take you to Trabert and Hoffert's—not Tiffany's, they're too big. And maybe we don't even have to go to the store. I'll have them send over their VP Susan Levinson with a nice selection. Pick out the one you want and then I'll take you down to Bridgeport. I'm buying one whole block—maybe it's a block you lived on once. I'm not very good with telling you how much I love you, but I can show you. I'm going to convert Bridgeport into apartments and shopping, keeping one apartment for us, of course. You know, I've never liked the idea of living up here in the ritzy Gold Coast, hope you won't mind us living there. What do you say, Clarissa? Clarissa, are you awake?"

He turned her limp body toward him.

"Oh, Clarissa."

He studied her in the moonlight—her eyes closed, her mouth curved in the gentlest half smile.

"Oh, Clarissa, have I got a surprise for you tomorrow morning."

THE NEXT MORNING, the telephone rang and Clarissa picked it up, half asleep.

"Hello?"

"Hello, Clarissa? Fred Tannenbaum."

She bolted awake. She sat up and then jerked her

head around to see the sprawling body of Conor James.

"Darling, you still there?"

"Sure, of course, I am, Fred. By the way, we really love the furniture. I wrote to you our thanks, but I only mailed it yesterday."

"Well, you'll have a chance to thank me in person," he said. The next few words were muffled with static and then the connection became clear again. "Darling, I'll talk fast because I've never been able to use the phone and fly at the same time."

"You mean drive."

"No, I mean fly. I'm on a Cessna plane and I'm nearly to Chicago. I should be coming into Miegs Field in three hours if they give me clearance."

Clarissa's heart started to pound.

Conor yawned and opened his eyes, giving her a level, dead-on stare.

"Uh, Fred, how, uh, nice of you to come up. Is it business or pleasure?"

"All pleasure, I hope. I've been doing a lot of thinking and I hope you're willing to forgive an old fool. Clarissa, I was absolutely wrong. You had a wonderful idea. Let's get married."

"Married?"

Conor slipped out of the sheets, naked, with a dark tan line where his jeans would cut into his hips. He walked out of the bedroom without a backward glance.

"Uh, Fred, I don't think…"

"Darling, I can't hear you."

"Fred, I was saying I don't think…"

"Clarissa, honey, the connection's getting worse."

"Fred, I said I don't…"

"Darling, I'll be there in three hours. I promise you I'll buy you the biggest diamond Tiffany's got and you tell your boy I'll do my best as a dad to him. You're never going to be poor again, darling, never going to be poor again in your life. And all I ask in return is the chance to be at your side. We'll grow old together—I'll just be doing it a little faster than you."

"Fred, I…"

"Clarissa, the connection's just too bad. I can't hear you at all. Bye, darling, I'll see you in just a few hours. I love you and the time apart has only made me realize just how much."

The line went dead.

Clarissa hung up, and threw off the sheets.

She reached the living room just as Conor was pulling on his boots.

How could I have been such a fool? he demanded of himself.

He stared at her, the woman he had loved, the woman he had spun a future for while she slept beside him. All the same features were there—the red hair, the pale amber eyes, the angel white skin now flushed with emotion. And yet, the beauty that yesterday had made him tender and loving now filled him with something akin to chilly disbelief.

How could I have been such a fool?

"You can't leave!" she exclaimed.

"I can and I have to. I can't stay to torture myself with this."

"You think I'm marrying Fred Tannenbaum."

"It's what you've been aiming for since the very first day I met you," Conor said with a calm he didn't possess. "I know that proper etiquette demands that I say best wishes to you and congratulations to him for having made this conquest, but I'm sure Miss Manners would forgive me if, in this case, the congratulations goes to the bride. Good job snaring him. And, as for Fred, best wishes for a happy future. However long he's got with you."

"I don't want him."

"Like hell you don't! I heard you on the phone with him."

"How was I supposed to know he was going to call?"

"I don't know the answer to that one. But I didn't hear you say 'Hi, Fred, I've got Conor James in bed with me and I love him.'"

"The connection was bad."

"It was good enough for a proposal," Conor said. "I heard it all the way in the living room. It came with a guarantee of diamonds."

She knew he hadn't heard everything Fred and she had said to each other, but she knew it would be a lie to deny the marriage proposal had come with a guarantee of diamonds.

"But I didn't say yes!"

"You didn't say no."

"I didn't get a chance."

"You didn't try."

"What's that supposed to mean?"

He pulled on both boots and stood.

Suddenly, Clarissa realized she was naked. She

reached down and pulled at the pile of her clothes, nabbing her blouse. She held it up for modesty.

Conor yanked it away from her. She stood, bare and startled, as he appraised her with angry, narrowed eyes. He put one hand against the wall in back of her, effectively pinning her in without touching her at all.

"Don't play modest with me now," he said, with rising fury. "How much of it was an act?"

"What are you talking about?"

"How much of it was a lie? The part about your ex-husband. The part about..."

She reddened.

"That part was true. It was all true."

"That part is a great line," he corrected. "It ought to rope those proposals right in. Makes a man feel like a hero in bed. That's the kind of thing that makes a woman look like—what did you call it?—wife material. Damn near worked with me."

"I trusted you!" she snapped.

"And I trusted you," Conor replied. "But it doesn't matter now. You want him. Or, if not him, someone like him. It's not the man, it's what's in his wallet—and I'm not talking about physical prowess. You want Fred Tannenbaum. He's yours. I feel sorry for the man and I hope he knows what he's getting into."

"I wanted you very much last night."

"But in the morning light, don't you want somebody with money?"

"Of course, I want a man with the ability to provide for me and my children, but I still, I can't help it, I...I love you."

"Don't want a nice house? Maybe an apartment just like this one?"

"Of course, I'd like that," Clarissa admitted, stumbling over her words, feeling as trapped in her confessions as if she were being cross-examined by the devil's own attorney. "But what woman wouldn't want those things?"

"What about a nice school for Tommy? And college tuition? What about a trip to Europe, to show him all the historical sites?"

"Of course, I'd want those things! What's so bad about that?"

"Then you can have them. You just can't have me with them."

"Then get out."

He shook his head with deadly calm.

"I was wrong about you, Clarissa. You're millionaire material through and through. Furs and pearls. Diamonds and caviar. That's you, baby."

"And I'm looking forward to getting accustomed to a life-style I deserve," she lied, hanging on to her pride by her fingernails.

He picked up his jacket from the hall console.

"If you're lucky, I'll come see you when you're married to Fred," he said coolly. "You can sneak me up the backstairs. You can tell me that I'm the only man who ever gives you pleasure. You can tell me that Fred doesn't satisfy you, that he never will. And we can playact that one for all it's worth."

Her eyes widened. He was taunting her with the most private, most intimate secret she carried within her. She had trusted him, had bared her soul—to say nothing of her body—and now he regarded her as having made it all up, as having lied to create some kind of sexual fantasy.

"Get out of here," she said, burning with anger. "I don't want to ever see you again."

"Oh, but you will, Clarissa, because what I gave you last night you're not going to get from Fred. Or from any other man, for that matter. Whether that story about you and your ex-husband was true or not."

She knew he might be right about the part that no other man could give her what he had. He had given her ecstasy, given her the shaking earth, given her a tingling sensation that lasted even until this morning.

But she also knew that she wouldn't want to see him again so long as she lived.

She knew she should tell him, right then and there, that she didn't want Fred, didn't want diamonds, didn't want trips to Europe, that she'd tell Fred the minute he got here that she couldn't marry him. And most of all, she should tell him, tell him that what they had shared last night was one of a kind for her.

It was all that mattered—she should do everything in her power to tell him so.

She wanted Conor. And she didn't care if he didn't come with a bank balance. She'd be willing to trust him, to trust that together they could build a life. They'd claw their way out of the debt she carried from her marriage and they'd slowly build a life of their own.

She wanted to drop to her knees and beg him to stay.

But something inside her stopped her in her tracks.

Something built inside over years of being shuttled from house to house, never really wanted, always resented as another mouth to feed. Something about being homeless and without a decent dress. Something about not knowing where her next meal was coming from. Something about being in a financial stranglehold because of her ex-husband's spending. Something about taking care of her son and securing a better future for him.

How dare Conor not understand? How dare he not comprehend why? Couldn't he see how terrifying the insecurity could be? How dare he think she had lied about…about the most intimate womanly thing.

"Get out," she said softly. "I don't need what you have to offer. I have to think of my future and Tommy's future. And as for Fred Tannenbaum? Fred's a wonderful man. He and I are going to be very happy."

"Oh, he's a wonderful man. But you're going to be a very rich, very cold, very lonely woman."

Without another word, he turned and left, slamming the front door behind him.

Clarissa stood for several minutes—shocked, stunned and shivering.

"At least I'll have a roof over my head and my children won't go hungry," she whispered.

Then she walked into the bedroom, grabbing a warm flannel nightgown from the dresser.

She got into bed and pulled the covers close to her neck.

But she couldn't stay there, not with the smell of their sex, of him, on her sheets.

So she got up and took a shower, scrubbing her skin

until she had washed away every trace of their love-making.

"Mrs. Clarissa Tannenbaum," she said to herself.

It didn't sound right.

"Mrs. Clarissa Tannenbaum," she repeated more loudly with as imperious a lilt as she could manage. "Mrs. Clarissa McShaunessy Tannenbaum!"

And she kept repeating all the ways her name would sound—Ms. Clarissa Tannenbaum, Mrs. Clarissa Tannenbaum, Mrs. Fred Tannenbaum, plain old Mrs. Tannenbaum—until it started, just started, to sound right.

Chapter Thirteen

"If you don't like it, Tiffany's will take it back," Fred cautioned. "You can pick out a new one. You can pick out as many new ones as you like. Think of that arrangement of rocks on your hand as just an opening offer, darling."

"Oh, no, it's very beautiful," Clarissa said numbly, staring at her left hand.

Which now felt very, very heavy.

"The biggest one there," Fred said, pointing at the middle stone of Clarissa's engagement ring. "The biggest one there is from Sri Lanka. It's eight carats and it has a C rating on color."

"Only a C?" Tommy queried.

"C is as clear as they come, Tommy. If you and your mom are going to let me buy lots of diamonds while we're married, you'll have to learn these things. You're going to have to learn your four Cs. Perfect cut, perfect clarity, perfect color, prefect... Well, you can see why they call it the four Cs."

"This looks like it's got lots of the Cs," Clarissa admitted, holding out her hand to the afternoon sunlight bursting into the living room. "And it's from Sri Lanka?"

"All the best diamonds come from there," Fred assured her. "Although some say the South African diamonds are just as good. You've got two small African ones there, one on each side of the big one. Four carats apiece."

The "small" ones still looked mighty big to Clarissa.

"What do you think, Tommy?"

Tommy got up from the couch and held out his mother's hand, inspecting the rocks.

"Nice and shiny, like diamonds should be," he said. "Sixteen carats altogether? Not bad."

"Glad you approve," Fred said with a good-natured smile.

"Did you know, Mr. Tannenbaum," Tommy regarded him with mature archness. "That by the time I go to college four years of higher education will cost over a quarter million dollars?"

Fred laughed and patted Tommy's cowlick.

"Don't you worry about that, son, you can go to any college you want. And it's Fred, not Mister, to you."

"All right, Fred. What about video games?" Tommy pressed. "Those can be expensive, but they're an important part of a boy's life. Training for the future, you know. A future with computers as a part of the workplace."

"Well, that's up to your mom." Fred ducked the question. "But the college is taken care of."

Tommy turned to Clarissa.

"I like this guy," he said. "Open the other boxes."

Clarissa looked at the array of gift boxes on the floor in front of her.

"Fred, you really shouldn't have done this."

"No, darling, I shouldn't have. But I felt like it. And when you have as much money as I do, you get to do things because you feel like it."

The engagement ring had been quite enough of a present to seal their marital bargain, but Fred Tannenbaum had felt like more. And he knew just what she'd like.

Clarissa opened two more boxes from Tiffany's to find three bangle bracelets with channel-set diamonds and sapphires, as well as a matching clustered diamond-and-sapphire earrings and necklace set. She put on the jewelry, at first tentatively, and then with growing delight.

It was hard not to get caught up in the Christmaslike atmosphere. Especially for a woman who had grown up without Christmases.

There were Chanel dresses—"I told them you were a small, but with curves"—luxurious shoes made by Italians whose names she couldn't pronounce, purses from Hermés with silk scarfs tied to their handles, and a Fendi cashmere stole that felt as soft and smooth as a baby's skin.

These were no hand-me-down clothes.

The last box had something even more precious: two key chains, each with a single brass key.

"They're to the main house," Fred explained. "One for you, one for Tommy. Although the security system has made keys a little obsolete. But I just wanted you to know you've both got a home of your own now."

Her eyes teared at his thoughtfulness.

A home was the most important gift Fred brought with him.

Also for Tommy, a navy blue suit which he hated and a gigantic pirate's castle Lego set which he loved. Clarissa promised him she'd help him put it together—it was larger than any other set Clarissa had ever bought him and it looked like a challenge.

"So, when are you two getting married?" Tommy asked.

"As soon as possible," Fred answered. "Maybe we could have a quick little ceremony up here and then have a larger, more formal do on my ranch."

"Will I get my own horse?" Tommy asked.

"Sure, you'll have your own horse and a heckuva lot of land," Fred replied. "Now, skedaddle while I talk to your Mom. Then I want to take you both to dinner. At the Club Ambassador—I have a hankering for a nice, juicy steak and a glass of champagne and that's the only place in town that does both things right. But you'll have to wear your suit. You're a gentleman now, Tommy."

"Oh, all right. If that's what it takes."

Tommy lugged his Lego box down the hall to his room.

Fred leaned back in the armchair and regarded Clarissa thoughtfully.

"Now, tell me I'm not rushing you into anything."

Clarissa had had a lot of time to think in the hours since Conor had stormed out of the apartment.

A lot of time for cool, quiet thinking.

Time for a reality check. A long overdue reality check.

She had studied her palm and had reviewed her options.

And had received a certified letter from creditors her ex-husband had evaded. The implacably determined letter laid out the consequences of nonpayment. Consequences that highlighted the folly of choosing her heart's desires over her well thought out plans.

Still, a man bringing lover's gifts made a mockery of her businesslike approach to matrimony.

"You're not rushing me into anything, Fred. I'm...actually worried about you."

"Me? I'm old enough to take care of myself. So, how 'bout it? Let's say we get married here very quietly, invite some of your friends?"

"Friends?"

"You must have some of those."

"I do. I do," Clarissa said.

She had a problem with that. She hadn't told her two closest friends, Hallie and Maggie, that her first marriage had broken up. Too embarrassed. She had grown up feeling like such a failure compared to them, Maggie now a super-model and Hallie a successful nurse. She had told them her marriage was rosy. Even when it wasn't. Because she never wanted their pity, never wanted them to worry, never wanted them to think she hadn't grown up into a woman who could take care of herself. Even coming to Chicago, she had purposely not called them—scared that they would want to help. And help some more. And help had been what Maggie and Hallie did a lot for her.

Now how could she call them and in one phone call announce that her supposedly perfect first marriage was over and a perfect second husband had been located?

On the other hand, they had been with her those many summers in Sabrina's tent. They would understand. And now that she had Fred's ring on her finger, she never had to feel as if she weren't as good as they were. She'd call them tomorrow morning, explain everything. Surely, they'd understand.

In the meantime, Fred was doing his own explaining...

"Darling, then I'm thinking we move on down to Oklahoma and plan something a little more formal for home?"

"Home?" Clarissa asked hollowly. Now things were really spinning out of control.

"Oklahoma. You remember, that panhandled state just north of Texas? The place where that key you're holding fits into? I can't drill for oil in downtown Chicago and I'm too old a dog to learn new tricks."

Oklahoma?

Remember that reality check, she thought to herself, this is no time to get misty eyed over Bridgeport.

"Will Tommy really get his own horse?"

Fred chuckled.

"He can have a hundred horses if he wants them. There's certainly enough on the ranch and he can pick any or all of them. I don't think Tommy will be unhappy. It's you I'm worried about. You don't like Tiffany's, do you?''

"Oh, no. I like Tiffany's."

"Don't like Chanel?"

"I love Chanel," she said, fingering the silk crepe of one of the dresses.

"You don't like Dolce and Gabbana?"

"Who?"

"The guys who made the shoes."

"No, the shoes are great. Even if I can't pronounce their names."

"You'll learn."

"I supposed I'll have to."

"Then what's the problem? You look like a mule stepped on your foot."

"Fred, I…"

She looked down at the sparkling jewels, at the fine clothes and around the room that was—because of this man—furnished. She heard her son singing a popular hip-hop song in the next room. She looked at Fred.

She remembered the sound of the door slamming as Conor left.

And she reminded herself that a reality check meant taking reality as it was. Not how she'd like it to be.

And so she shoved down every smidgen of regret. About the man who had left the apartment only hours before Fred arrived. Conor James had his carefree, footloose life to lead—and she had her own path in life to follow.

"Fred, before you commit to marrying me, you'd better hear what I have to tell you."

"Darling, I think I'm going to beat you to the

punch,'' he said kindly. ''You want to tell me you had a plan to find a rich, adorable husband like me.''

Clarissa stared at him in amazement.

''You knew?''

''You don't get to be my age, with my money, without a woman or two having a scheme to hog-tie you onto the altar. I happen to have been the lucky target of yours.''

''You don't mind?''

''Mind? Oh, no. Some women want to be movie stars, some women want to be doctors, some women want to be astronauts. You want to be a wife and mother and you want to do it with a little job security. I can't blame you for that. Now, why don't you dress for dinner? Pick one of the Chanel numbers.''

Clarissa knew which one she liked best—the pink silk knit with the black ribbon finishing. She thanked him again, gave him a tentative kiss on his forehead and headed for the bedroom.

''Oh, Clarissa,'' Fred called after her.

''Yes?''

She looked back at him.

''You'll come to love me,'' he reassured her. ''It won't be fireworks, but it'll be all right. I'm not a hard man to live with. I forget to take off my boots when I come in the house if someone doesn't remind me and I'm terrible about remembering birthdays. But I'll be good to you. I already have a passel of lawyers— estate and tax guys—figuring out how to ensure that Tommy goes to college and you never have to worry. And I won't ask for anything…intimate until you're ready. Really ready.''

She leaned against the doorjamb.

"Fred, I'll do my best to be a good wife to you," she promised, her heart breaking at his earnestness.

"Then let's go out and celebrate."

They exchanged shy smiles and Clarissa took her dress into the bedroom.

Chanel.

Think of it!

Clarissa McShaunessy in a real Chanel dress.

Not even "gently used."

Not even something Hallie or Maggie bought and then gave to her, thinking she would believe them when they said that she was doing them the favor taking it because they had lost the receipt and the store wouldn't take it back....

She slipped the dress over her shoulders and looked in the mirror. With the diamonds at her ears and on her throat, with pretty bangles on her wrists— Why, she looked...like a million dollars!

She felt the stirrings of being pampered and spoiled and cared for. It was a strange feeling, foreign and welcome at the same time. She hadn't felt this good since...

She closed her eyes.

She wouldn't, couldn't look at the bed.

Not at the bed.

Not where another man had pampered her, had spoiled her, had cared for her...had loved her.

She wasn't going to look back. It wouldn't do any good if she did. He was gone. And even if he hadn't left, she would have had to kick him out eventually.

He was a ne'er-do-well. Would never amount to

anything. Disdained "regular" jobs. Needed to grow up.

Sure, he had made love with a tenderness and an expertise that left her shaking even now when she was six hours—and a lot of thinking—out of bed.

But a woman couldn't eat on passion, couldn't provide for her kids on passion, couldn't give her kids a place to live on passion.

She looked at her palm, at the divergent wrinkles on the otherwise smooth, ivory skin. Two different futures. Two very different men.

She had just barely avoided a disaster. If she had thought only with her body and not with her brains—she might be Conor's woman.

She bit her lip to make herself stop thinking that being Conor's woman wouldn't have been so bad.

Tommy walked into her room.

"Is Conor going to still baby-sit for us?"

Clarissa shook her head. "No, darling, he isn't."

"That's too bad. He was a great baby-sitter. I liked him."

"Do you like Fred?"

"Sure. He's all right. Which guy do you like better?"

"They're not the same," Clarissa explained. "Fred's a husband. Conor's a...well, it's not the same."

"Okay," Tommy said. "Is it time for dinner yet?"

She nodded and he said he'd go get his navy suit. Clarissa watched him go and marveled at how quickly he could bounce back from losing his...

"Aw, he's just the baby-sitter," Clarissa said angrily and jerked open the chest of drawers, looking for a pair of stockings that didn't have a run.

Clarissa stared at Tommy's hamburger and fries.

Why don't I get to order from the children's menu? she wondered, as she looked down at her own plate, a mélange of porcini mushrooms and truffles sautéed in what looked to be motor oil.

Something completely unpronounceable, supposed to be the Club Ambassador's signature dish.

She'd rather have hamburger and fries.

Oh, no, you don't! Clarissa pursed her lips.

Don't you dare think of him! Don't you dare think of hamburgers and hot dogs and regular Cokes and blue jeans and Disney movies and hot, hot, hot kisses. And million dollar bets that will never be collected on.

"Darling? Are you all right?" Fred asked.

Clarissa swallowed. And tilted her chin up at a you-bet-I-am angle.

"I'm just great, Fred. Why don't you pour me a glass of champagne?"

ONCE CLARISSA MADE UP her mind that she was going to marry Fred Tannenbaum, she promised herself to never look back.

First, she called Hallie and explained haltingly that she wouldn't be trying again with her first husband. Funny, Hallie hadn't been the slightest bit surprised. Then Clarissa explained she was marrying the real love of her life, which did surprise Hallie.

She took Hallie to lunch at the Pump Room to catch up on things and then Hallie stayed to go with Clarissa for a quick trip to Tiffany's—which was becoming Clarissa's favorite store.

"I'll have one of these and one of those and one of that and throw in this one, too," Clarissa said to the manager who had been instructed by Fred to open an unlimited charge account for her. She pointed to several other trays of jewelry and made selections from each.

"What are you doing?" Hallie demanded, twisting a lock of her brown hair nervously. "You just picked out more jewelry than the Queen of England owns!"

"Just a little shopping," Clarissa explained, only a little defensive. "Wouldn't you like one of these? As a present from me and Fred."

She pointed to the array of glittering jewels on the black velvet cloth which the manager had pulled out for her.

"Would you like me to box them and deliver them to your apartment, Miss McShaunessy?" he asked.

"Yes, please," Clarissa said. "So, Hallie, at least a tennis bracelet, okay?"

Hallie stared at Clarissa, openmouthed.

"Do you really love him in your heart?" she whispered. "Because you seem awfully frantic for someone in love."

Clarissa looked at her friend. Oh, how it hurt to lie. But if she told the truth just once to Hallie, everything would fall apart.

And then she'd be Clarissa McShaunessy—orphaned, alone, a hand-me-down girl—all over again. She was nearly, but not quite, Mrs. Clarissa Tannenbaum.

"I love Fred more than I've loved any man on earth," she said firmly. "Besides, remember how Sabrina promised I'd marry a millionaire?"

"That's right!" Hallie shrieked. "Oh my gosh, maybe Sabrina's a real seer! I just thought of her as the nice old lady who lived in the apartment above the drugstore, but she really saw the future for you. And, Clarissa, you deserve so much love and you are so loving a person. And to have him be a millionaire, too. I'm so happy for you!"

Maggie had been slightly less impressed.

Fred had flown Clarissa and Tommy to Texas in his Cessna to visit with Maggie for the day. What a difference from the times Tommy and Clarissa had taken the long, hot bus ride to visit Hallie's super-model cousin.

"You've never been a very good liar," Maggie said, with characteristic bluntness. "You don't love him."

Clarissa colored.

"Maggie, you've already gotten everything you've ever wanted out of life," she said, feeling tears welling in her eyes. "But, try to understand, other than having Tommy, I've never even come close. I want a home, a family, some security. Fred is all that, and more."

Maggie instantly softened.

"I want you to be happy," she said, hugging Clarissa. "Are you really happy?"

Clarissa thought of the time that Maggie had pulled strings to get Clarissa's husband a job—a job he had managed to blow in less than a week. She thought of how Maggie had paid the hospital bill when Tommy had been born—calling it just a little baby gift, but Clarissa always knew it was charity. She loved Maggie and knew that Maggie loved her. But, for once, Clarissa wanted to prove she was a friend who could stand on her own two feet and that she wasn't just a burden.

"I have my millionaire," she said and she reminded Maggie of Sabrina's prediction.

"She also said that Hallie would marry that dreadful boy next door and that isn't going to happen."

"Maybe it's hocus-pocus. But I'm engaged."

"Are you happy?"

Clarissa sighed.

"When I marry Fred Tannenbaum and Fred becomes Tommy's father, he'll give Tommy so much. Things that I could never give Tommy in a million years."

It was a phrase that she would repeat often during the visit, more to reassure herself than to ease Maggie's worried look.

Maggie only challenged Clarissa once.

"Don't put too much store in money, Clarissa," she said as the two friends sat beside the cowboy-boot-shaped pool at Jake MacIntyre's ranch, looking on as Jake's twin nephews and Tommy splashed and frolicked in the water. Jake was the down-home cowboy smitten—if Clarissa was any judge—with Maggie. The model's blond hair was pulled back in a casual ponytail and her maillot was sleek and shiny. "It really isn't the key to happiness. It's family that counts. Friends. Being with someone you love with all your heart and soul."

Clarissa had no answer for her friend's unspoken question—did she love Fred that way?

ON THURSDAY AFTERNOON, Clarissa's apartment was the site of what was supposed to be a very small, very intimate wedding.

"How many people are out there?" Clarissa asked, looking down at the vanity, which was covered with a week's worth of jewelry from her husband-to-be. And a congratulatory telegram from Maggie.

"A gazillion," Tommy answered confidently, peeking out the bedroom window. "Hey, there's Michael Jordan."

"Get a grip on yourself, Tommy, this is the way it's going to be from now on. You'll have to get used to seeing celebrities and keeping your tongue off the floor when you do."

"I like it."

"Don't get starstruck."

Clarissa pulled at the skirt of her Vera Wang dress and walked to the bedroom door with the mincing steps of a geisha girl. Pencil-skirted wedding dresses were the hottest thing and the New York designer had flown in just yesterday to fit Clarissa.

Only problem was a woman couldn't walk in this dress, and heels only made it worse. And forget running, playing ball, or falling over and getting up without assistance. Not that any of these things were being planned. No—just a small wedding, Clarissa thought.

Still, it was a beautiful dress. Drop-dead gorgeous and covered with minuscule pearls and crystal beads.

Clarissa sidled up to Tommy, opening the bedroom door just a crack to see into the hallway.

Stunned, she closed the door and leaned against it, panicked.

"Tommy, I think Fred must have two hundred close, intimate friends. How am I supposed to go out there?"

There was a knock on the door and someone said, "Two minutes, Miss McShaunessy."

Clarissa took her son's hand in her own.

"Am I doing the right thing?" she asked aloud.

"How would I know? I'm just a kid."

Clarissa smiled, knowing just how much she loved him.

"Will you be happy in Oklahoma?" she asked.

"I'll be happy anywhere, as long as I'm with you and we have a place to stay."

"That ranch is going to be an awfully great place to stay."

"Yeah."

"All right, then, I guess it's time for us to go," she said. "Can you get my flowers from the vanity? I want to conserve my energy. Walking in this dress is like running with a sheet wrapped around your legs."

He got her the flowers and she adjusted his bow tie.

"I'm very proud of you, Tommy," she said. "I think you're going to grow up to be a very wonderful man."

"And you're real beautiful, Mom," he said levelly. "You look like a million, no, a billion, no, a gazillion bucks."

She kissed him, but he pushed her away with an

"aw, Mom, I'm too old for this," and she couldn't wrestle him to the ground and tickle him like she would ordinarily because she was chained to the dress.

Besides, they heard the first stirrings of the bridal march.

"Ready, Mom?"

"As ready as I'm ever going to be."

He held out his arm for her. She took it, thinking about how one day, very soon, he would be tall enough that she wouldn't have to look down to meet his eyes.

And then she'd have Fred. Her husband. They would have a lot of time to grow into marriage. A very long time.

They began the long, slow march to the judge and the groom who waited in the living room.

The mayor and his entourage stood by the entry to the kitchen. He smiled at her and reached out to shake her hand—though they had never met.

Two Hollywood directors, the junior senator from Illinois and the owner of the Chicago Bears each gave her a thumbs-up as they clustered together at the hall console. A renowned gossip columnist stopped slurping his martini long enough to nod a hello.

And in addition to the celebrities were the regular people—if you could call the millionaires and billionaires of Chicago society regular.

And every one of them here for Fred Tannenbaum.

In fact, the only person from her side of the aisle she could see was Sabrina with Gervase on her shoulder, both looking pretty unhappy considering that Clarissa was about to get married on Sabrina's recommendation. Hallie hadn't been able to come because of an emergency at the hospital.

But there was Conor, standing by the balcony door—wearing jeans, of course, Clarissa noted sourly.

The man didn't know enough to wear a suit when he was crashing somebody's wedding, she thought.

Wait a minute! Conor's here? Clarissa stumbled on the hem of her gown, but Tommy steadied her.

She looked into Conor's eyes. Darkened teal blue, narrowed sardonically. She put a hand to the beaded neckline of her gown, as if to check that her dress was still there, because he sure looked as if it weren't. He was reminding her, with just an arch of his eyebrow, of the intimacy they had shared.

She wondered, with rising horror, if anyone around them could sense that intimacy as well.

She couldn't let him get to her.

She raised her chin and forced herself to stare into the crowd surrounding the judge, trying to find Fred.

How dare Conor crash her wedding! How dare he come here and taunt her—yes, taunt her—with his provocative stare! How dare he remind her of...

That night.

Everything about that night came back to her in a rush that nearly made her lose her balance. That night when she discovered that there was passion for her. That there was a soul mate who could open up her body's secrets. That there was somebody who understood everything about her—even the scared little girl who thought no one loved her.

He might have thought she lied, that it was simply a game of seduction.

But it was no game for her.

It was her life.

It was her truth.

It was everything about her.

She continued toward the judge and met Fred's eyes. Fred was a nice man. A caring and generous man. One who would take care of her and her son with every ounce of his energy and with every dollar to his name.

And all she had to give up, give up for a lifetime, was an unemployed no-account rogue who had just been toying with her heart anyway.

Chapter Fourteen

"Dearly beloved, we are gathered here today to honor and celebrate the joining of these two dear and wonderful people—Fred Tannenbaum and Clarissa McShaunessy—in holy matrimony."

The black-robed judge was renowned for his handling of one of the many celebrated trials of the decade. And it was no wonder, the way that he commanded the group of luminaries and other guests, the way that he gave a grave and yet celebratory air to the ceremony. His eyes were small and dark, and his cheeks shook like gelatin when he talked.

"This decision to marry is not to be taken lightly," he warned. "Nor is it to be done in haste."

Clarissa looked over her shoulder, trying to find Conor. She knew she shouldn't, but it was like telling Tommy that his mosquito bite would feel better if he didn't scratch it.

Fred gently brought her back to her senses with just the touch of his hand on her elbow.

But still, she saw Conor out of the corner of her eye. He sat on the balcony, his back to the windows. Why was he here? How did he get in—when security was so tight that three reporters from national tabloids had already been thrown out?

Was he unhappy? she wondered. Did he wish that she was his? Would either of them take back any of their angry words if they were given a chance?

But, of course, in this love match there were no second chances.

Standing here in front of the judge who looked as if he could as easily sentence her to life imprisonment as he could officiate at her wedding made Clarissa realize how final this decision to marry Fred Tannenbaum actually was.

She glanced at Sabrina, standing by herself in the corner. Not exactly by herself, since she had Gervase on her shoulder. Gervase, who scattered cracker crumbs on any guest who was foolish enough to come within three feet of him.

Second chances.

Sabrina had said there were no second chances for her, not at this time in her life. That whatever she chose would haunt her or please her—but it would be final.

No second chances.

Is this what Sabrina meant?

Clarissa closed her eyes and all the pressure and stress of the past weeks rained down on her. She was a strong woman, used to adversity, used to squelching her feelings if the situation required it, used to holding up for appearances sake, if necessary.

But, suddenly, this was too big for her.

Too big, too final, too irrevocable.

She was marrying one man and hopelessly—admit it, she told herself—hopelessly in love with another.

The beautiful orchids slipped from her hands. The room seemed to recede to a faraway place. She heard, as if from a distance, the gasp of the crowd, the quiet but urgent concern in Fred's voice, the judge's stern attempts to restore order.

Fred took her in his arms.

"Darling, what's wrong?"

"Fred, I'm so sorry...I just...I just don't know what I'm doing anymore," she whispered, wearily looking up at him.

He touched her lip to quiet her and nodded grimly. Then, firmly taking her arm, he guided her through the sea of shocked faces.

From a distant place, Clarissa could hear the judge saying, "Folks, be calm. We'll just be a minute. No need to panic. Order, order, order. Could we please just have some order?"

Fred got her into the bedroom and closed the door. Clarissa immediately slipped off her high heels and slumped down on the bed in a defeated heap.

"Fred, I can't explain all this," she said. "But maybe I'm not who I think I am."

"If you don't mind telling me, who are you then?" Fred asked, sitting on the edge of the vanity seat.

"I thought I was cool and sophisticated and pragmatic and rational and a lot stronger than I really am."

"I thought you are pretty much all those things," Fred said. "But who is it that you are if you aren't who you and I think you are?"

"I'm just a scared little girl who thought if she

could just take away all the risks in life, everything would be all right.''

"Risks are always there."

"I'm figuring that out."

"I always find that when I'm the most scared that's when I have to make the choice that carries the most risk, the most danger. It's how I've made my life and my fortune. Give it your best shot, Clarissa, make your choice.''

"Fred, it's not a matter of choice. It's a matter of destiny. I can't marry you.''

"I figured as much."

"You knew?"

"I knew from the moment you walked out of the bedroom. You had a look on your face like a little bunny rabbit about to be hit by a car.''

He came to sit next to her on the bed and put his arms around her as she started to cry.

"I'm sorry, Fred."

"I know you are."

"Are you mad at me? You'd have the right to be."

"No, not mad. Not mad at you. I've lived long enough and gone through enough that I know when people have tried their best to do right by me. And you tried pretty hard there. You're too honorable, that's all. Too honorable to do something a little calculating, a little mercenary—like marrying a man you don't really love just because he's rich.''

"I don't think of myself as all that honorable," Clarissa said, thinking of the weeks she had spent trying her darndest to land a wealthy husband. "I just think I'm not millionaire material.''

He looked her up and down.

"Don't sell yourself short. You look pretty good in that dress. You know how to use your silverware. And you caught on pretty quick about C-quality diamonds."

"No, Fred, I'm not millionaire material. I'm working class through and through. Oh, you can take back all those diamonds and the dresses and everything else. I like the necklace Tommy made from macaroni just fine. And I'm better off in jeans and cowboy boots. And I think I like hamburgers better than caviar. And I don't really want a ranch or a palace or a mansion or even an apartment on the Gold Coast, so you'd better see if the furniture store will take back all this stuff you got us."

"But, darling, the whole point of money is that you can choose what you want to do. All money is, is freedom. We can go down to the Gap right now and buy a pair of jeans. What do you think I wear on the ranch? And I don't eat caviar all that much. I'm pretty partial to macaroni and cheese and I think steaks do a man fine."

"It's not just that."

"Oh," he said, regarding her thoughtfully. And then suddenly he had a revelation. "Why, Clarissa McShaunessy, I think you've fallen in love."

Clarissa nodded glumly.

"I think I have, too."

"Tell me all about the lucky guy," he said kindly, recovering from heartache with the same speed with which he had recovered from the many but short-term downturns and catastrophes of his business.

Clarissa grabbed a tissue and wiped the tears from under her eyes.

"I've fallen in love with a louse who won't get a job, who doesn't even have a savings account, and who's probably never owned a suit in his life."

"Sounds like a real winner."

"He is. That Conor James is a real piece of work. He's a lousy, no-good, rotten…"

Fred did a double take.

"Did you say Conor James? You've fallen in love with Conor James?"

"Yeah," Clarissa said, pulling off her veil and letting the toile and pressed-flower confection float to the floor. "The jerk crashed the wedding and didn't even have enough simple respect for the ceremony to wear a tie and suit jacket. He's so damned independent, so arrogant, so cocky."

"That's Conor for you," Fred said in a barely there whisper. "I'm not sure I've ever seen him in a tie or a jacket, either."

"Why did I have the terrible luck to fall for such a guy?" Clarissa wondered aloud. "I just hope I have the strength to stick to my guns. I can only see him if things change. The only way we've got a future at all is if he gets a job. A real job. And starts living life a little more responsibly."

"Wait right here," Fred said, leaving her just as she leaned back and put her head on the pillow.

She felt worn out, hungry and as despondent as a condemned woman should feel.

TOMMY AND CONOR were playing hearts at the wrought iron table on the balcony. Tommy was winning. Fred sat down at the table. Conor didn't look up.

"Conor, you and I go back a long way," Fred said. "I remember a few deals we did together."

"Yeah," Conor said miserably. "And congratulations to you. If you go for tall, leggy redheads with cold, cold...hearts," he concluded, throwing down the queen of hearts.

"I've got an eight," Tommy chirped, oblivious to Conor's dark mood.

Fred picked up the play Tommy made and replaced the card with another from Tommy's hand.

A devastating card—the king of hearts.

Tommy was now on the brink of winning.

"Conor, I think the congratulations should be extended to you," Fred said in a low voice.

Conor reached across the table and clamped his hands tightly over Tommy's ears. "Why the congrats? Because I managed to evade her gold-digging plot? Because I'm not the one who's going to be financing her every whim?"

Fred shook his head. "No, the congratulations are because she wants you."

Conor let go of Tommy's ears.

"How come I never get to hear the good stuff?" Tommy wondered.

Conor stared at Fred and then back at the crowd milling around the living room.

"She wants me?"

"Yeah, she specifically asked for the guy without enough class to wear a tie and jacket to a wedding."

"You mean the wedding's off?"

"I just called the Club Ambassador and told them to set up the bar for a cocktail party that thought it was a wedding," Fred said. "This apartment will be empty in less than five minutes."

"The Club Ambassador?" Tommy whined. "Do I have to go? I don't want to wear this suit anymore."

"No, my young friend. We're going to see the new Jean-Claude Van Damme movie. It's playing at four."

"Cool."

"We've got just enough time to go to McDonald's if you hurry and get out of that monkey suit. If you're anything like your mom, you've been very patient with me for the last week."

"Just a little," Tommy admitted, and ran through the French doors to the apartment.

Conor shuffled and laid the cards out on the table. "I don't want her," he said.

"Don't let your pride get in the way, Conor. You've never done that in business. Don't start doing it in love."

"She's trouble."

"Only to a man who doesn't understand her."

"She's a gold digger!"

"She's a pretty miserable excuse for a gold digger," Fred countered calmly. "She's sitting on the bed crying her eyes out over you and she's giving up marriage to me—and I'll have you know that *Fortune* magazine will be listing me as one of the twenty richest bachelors in next month's issue. You're in, too—several million dollars in net worth behind me, I'd like to point out."

"So let her pick up her copy of *Fortune* at the newsstand and weep over how she let me slip through her diamondless little fingers.''

"Maybe I haven't made all this clear," Fred said, gathering the cards. "She has no idea now that you're not the delightful unemployed freewheeling no-account you've presented yourself as. But she still wants you. She's the only woman in America who's after you for…just plain you. I'd take her. But, I was going to take her anyhow.''

"So why are you giving her up?" Conor asked. "Because you could go right back in that room and persuade her—dangle a few diamonds in front of her, maybe the papers for a trust fund for Tommy. Promise her security. Tell her she'd never have to worry about the rent money again. Tell her I'm not interested and that you're the last man left.''

"Maybe I could, but maybe I think I couldn't. Maybe I think I shouldn't. Besides, she's got you to give her all those things. And a few more things that a gentleman shouldn't discuss.''

Conor shook his head and emitted a harsh oath.

"Oh, Conor, you've got it bad," Fred said, shaking his head. "I don't think you've ever fallen in love before. Feels a little like getting whacked by a hammer on the side of your head, don't you think?''

"Yeah, but I still have the willpower to not do any-thing about such a condition. Like inviting the hammer to hit me again and again.''

Fred shook his head. "I married my high school sweetheart and I can't imagine how my life would have turned out if I hadn't had June at my side. She was my rock, she was what made life beautiful, she pulled me through the tough times and partied at my side through the good.''

''But June took you when you were just a struggling rancher. Clarissa doesn't want me. She wants a rich husband.''

''She could have had me. My millions don't do anything for her, and my greenbacks are just as good as yours.''

''Would she marry me if I was poor?'' Conor demanded.

''You could go right in there now and find out the answer to that question.''

''And when do I tell her that I'm not poor?''

''You don't. Don't shatter her illusions.''

Conor stood up.

Fred smiled with the satisfaction of a man who has done a good thing.

''Remember, Conor, she doesn't fall in love with millionaires.''

The two men shook hands silently.

As Conor strode through the apartment, the mayor's entourage was sorting through their distinctly similar black overcoats. The two Hollywood directors had already left, the owner of the Bears was rummaging through the hall closet for his wife's wrap, and the junior senator from Illinois was on the kitchen phone asking the baby-sitter if she would mind staying a few extra hours. Conor helped two blue-haired ladies with their wraps and tipped the departing bartenders twenty bucks apiece.

Then he surveyed the nearly empty apartment.

Hmmm, a four o'clock movie.

Assuming Jean-Claude Van Damme hadn't lost his touch, Conor figured he had about five hours altogether. If Fred was buying dinner for Tommy.

Five hours. Only five more hours of being Conor James, bad boy good-for-nothing who stole an honorable gold digger's heart.

He took a deep breath as he stood before the bedroom door. He had never been more sure of himself. She wanted him. He was going to open that door and she would be his if he wanted.

Was she a cold-blooded calculator who wanted money, diamonds, furs and caviar? Or was she the tender woman he made love to, whose tears of joy and wonder had made everything to his jaded mind seem new?

He'd find out.

He opened the door.

She sat on the bed in that impossible dress and looked up at him. Two hot circles of red dappled her cheeks and tears welled in her eyes.

"Baby," he said, confident and proud.

"Don't come in here unless you're willing to play by my rules," she said smartly.

Chapter Fifteen

"Oh, really?" Conor replied, letting the door close behind him.

"Yes, really," Clarissa said, standing and wishing she had on her heels. He really was too tall for her to order about.

"I'm going to play by your rules?"

"Yes, you are," she said, hoping that he couldn't see how her confidence faltered. "Rule number one. You have to get a real job."

He started to laugh.

It made her mad. He had no right, absolutely no right to laugh. This was a serious situation. She had just thrown away her future, her son's future…and all she was trying to do was salvage what was left.

"You have to get a job," she repeated.

"All right."

His eyes twinkled mockingly.

"I'm not joking," she said sternly.

"I'm not, either. I'll get a 'real' job. If it's all that important to you."

"And a savings account," Clarissa said, wagging a

finger at him. "Ten percent of your paycheck goes into savings. And that's before taxes."

"Passbook account?"

"Yes."

"Oh, Clarrisa, no. Those things get terrible interest. We could do much better in the stock market."

"How would you know?" Clarissa demanded. "You've never had two pennies to put together, much less enough to gamble on the market."

He shrugged.

"Is that it?"

"No, there's more. I want you to buy a suit."

"You drive a very hard bargain."

"Don't be so cocky."

"That's how I am," he said. "And you want me...how I am. Fine, I'll get a suit. Then you'll have the problem of how to get me to wear it. Now, what's the last rule?"

"You owe me an apology."

"For wha...?"

Their eyes met, and she willed herself to keep her gaze steady. At first, his eyes held all of his usual rugged challenge.

And then, in an instant, he remembered himself and what she was talking about.

And he knew he was at fault.

"I wasn't lying," she said softly. "I wasn't lying, Conor."

He took her full measure.

"You weren't, were you?"

"No. A woman doesn't lie about that sort of thing. You were...my first. And that night was my first time.

Now, maybe everything I did seemed so mercenary that you might have thought I was calculating about making love. Just as calculating as I seemed about everything else. But I wasn't calculating about that. I trusted you with something very private, and I didn't like having it thrown up in my face."

"Then, you're right. And I'm very sorry."

She forgave him.

"All right, stop looking so down," she said. "Apology accepted. You can go back to being Conor James now. You remember him—the unemployed no-account who's far too cocky for his own good. Don't you have a few conditions you want to impose?"

"I sure do. If I'm going to have to get a job and save money and wear a tie, I'd better get something in return."

"Like what?"

He circled around her slowly. She felt uncomfortably on display, though she was covered modestly with yards of silk, of pearls, of sequins and beads. Two seconds ago, she had been in charge, laying down the law.

Now, suddenly, he was in charge and Clarissa could only shiver with a combination of fear and animal anticipation.

"Now, here are my rules," he said at her neck. "No dresses that are this hard to get off."

She gasped as he traced a lazy line down the back of her dress.

"I want you always easy to...reach," he said. "Understand?"

She nodded, suddenly too overcome to protest. It was hot, suddenly very hot in the bedroom.

"How many buttons does this thing have?" Conor asked.

"Vera Wang, the designer, said over one hundred and fifty."

"Well, limit yourself to two or three from now on," he ordered, and with one swift movement he ripped the dress in two and it fell in a shudder to the floor.

Buttons rolled under the bed, behind the dresser, across the Aubusson throw rug, twirling like tops on the hardwood floor.

"Conor! My God, that dress cost Fred fifteen thousand dollars! He's going to kill us."

"I think not," Conor said calmly. "Now, you want to hear rule number two?"

Her eyes met his and even as she revelled in his appraisal of her body, her hands still moved to cover herself, to pull at the lacy edges of the matching Natori bra and panties.

"You're to go back to wearing cotton," he said, reaching around her to unclasp the scanty bra. "Simple cotton underwear. Regular people underwear. My kind of underwear. Your kind of underwear. Even with safety pins."

He held up the bra and then the ribbon of lace, delicate pearls and sheer silk disappeared in his fist. His eyes were drawn to her breasts. Clarissa felt the straining ache of her nipples and moved to cover them. Her own touch, under his feral gaze, did nothing for modesty and everything for heat.

He dropped the bra and took each of her hands in

his own, holding her arms out wide from her body, and then he leaned down to kiss each berry-colored nipple. Throwing her head back she strained upward to meet his mouth—her back arched, high on tiptoes. He teased each breast with kisses, at once gentle and then with growing heat.

Then, abruptly, he denied himself, denied them both—relinquishing her to her short, begging cry.

"Rule number three—we're living in Bridgeport."

"It's the only place in Chicago we could afford," she said raggedly. "Until you get a job, we're going to be living on my paycheck from the Latin School, remember?"

He reached down to her panties.

"Ready to give up diamonds and pearls?"

He guided her down and stood at the edge of the bed, between her knees.

"Yes, Conor, I am," she said, annoyed. "You've already figured that out."

"Ready to give up mansions and furs and fancy clothes?"

"Conor, you know all that. Stop reminding me."

He unbuttoned his shirt.

"Then maybe I had better show you again how I'm going to make this all worthwhile. For both of us."

Suddenly, something distracted her. Maybe a woman's laughter, maybe the sound of a glass being touched at its rim by another. Something from outside their private world.

"Conor, you can't do this! We've got guests out there! The mayor, the senator, all of Chicago society is standing this moment in the living room!"

He threw his shirt in the direction of the closet.

"They've left. Gone to the Club Ambassador for drinks."

He unsnapped his jeans.

"What about Fred? What about Tommy?"

"They went to the movies together."

"What about Sabrina?"

He paused. "Sabrina?"

"The older woman. Wearing gypsy clothes. Came with a monkey. She's a palm reader."

"Oh, Sabrina. Last I looked, she was reading Fred's fortune. Told him a dark, exotic woman of mature years was coming into his life and that she would know all the love secrets of the Orient. Fred invited her to the movies with them. I think Fred's a little enchanted."

"So, what are we going to do?"

"Oh, Clarrisa, you know exactly what we're going to do," he said, leaning down to cover her body with his own. "I'm going to owe you another million dollars when we're through."

"Some day I'll try to collect."

"I always make good on my bets."

"Now you're going to tell me that gambling is another of your vices?"

"No, but gambling on you is. And after I make love to you, then I want a hamburger."

"A hamburger sounds good. I haven't eaten since yesterday so that I could fit into the dress," she said, and then she remembered. "Are you buying? I'm down to my last dollar."

"Yeah, I'm buying. And then after lunch, we're going down to the courthouse to get married. Because I won't stand for you chasing after any other millionaires."

"Married?" She swallowed. "I thought you weren't the marrying kind."

"I'm not. But I don't know any other way to keep you."

She glanced one last time at her palm before his kisses distracted and entranced her. Her future couldn't be that bad—he was at his core a good man, kind to Tommy, a tender and yet fiery lover. And maybe he'd learn to stay at a job and she could manage the money, what little they'd have.

Besides, she couldn't get him out of her system. She had to have him.

As he reached to touch the core of her, the tender pink bud that set off her excitement, she decided there was no point in doing anything other than embracing her future, whatever loving Conor James would bring. She felt the blood rush to her head, shoving away all reason and thought, and she gave herself to him, to pleasure, to passion.

And the last thought before she lost all reason was why.

Why, oh why, did she have to fall for a louse like Conor James?

CLARISSA SAT at the vanity wrapped in one of Conor's shirts and sporting a regular pair of white cotton panties and matching racer-back tank top. Her hair, made tousled and tangled by their energetic lovemaking, was pulled back by a rubber band. She chewed the eraser of her pencil and made notes on the pad of paper on her lap.

"I'm still on hold with the bank," she said.

She turned around to look at Conor.

As sated as a well-fed lion, he lay propped against the pillows, his arms folded behind his head. His chest was smooth and muscular. He looked at her boldly.

And with a smile that let her know that she had been totally and completely his—and he enjoyed it.

Obviously not as concerned as she was with their long-term financial prospects.

Though they had made love just in the past two hours, Clarissa still felt a rising tide of wanting.

Terrible to depend on a man for this feeling, a feeling so new that she wondered each time he brought her to climax if she was losing her grip on the earth or if the sky was coming down. Terrible to depend on a man who looked as if he wasn't getting out of bed anytime soon.

Or maybe it wasn't so bad.

He gave her love and a security and an inner peace that she had never known. In his arms, she felt a happiness, a contentment that had never been hers. She knew that through every struggle of their coming lives, he would give her strength and humor to endure. No, not quite. Her whole life she had been "enduring"— he would give her enjoyment.

She could enjoy her life, not merely endure it.

For that, maybe she should forgive him his little faults.

Like the fact that he had no money, no prospects,

no work ethic, and probably no intention of changing for her.

Regardless of what rules she laid out.

"I'm trying to find out how much money we have altogether," Clarissa explained to him, though he merely smirked. "You might not believe this, but we can't afford to live like this. I've got to get us a place to live."

"Bridgeport. A good place to raise a family. An up-and-coming neighborhood."

"Fine. Bridgeport," Clarissa agreed, not relishing the idea of returning to her old neighborhood with a scoundrel of a husband. Doing it in diamonds had seemed so much nicer. "It's going to take a lot to make the old neighborhood up-and-coming, so maybe we'll be urban pioneers. I've got just about nothing in my checking account and it's a week and a half until payday. Do you have any money at all in your pockets?"

He lifted up the sheet and stared down at himself. He winked suggestively.

"You could come and find out," he offered.

Clarissa stared heavenward.

He was incorrigible!

"Ms. McShaunessy, sorry for the wait." The teller came back on the line. "We show your balance at three million dollars and thirty-two cents as of an hour ago."

"Huh?"

"Three million and thirty-two cents."

"There must be some mistake. I know where the thirty-two cents comes from. I was expecting that, although I admit I was hoping my math was wrong. But how'd I end up with all those millions?''

The teller giggled.

''When the bank makes a mistake in the customer's favor, I don't think I've ever heard the customer complain before. Most folks would just take the money.''

''I'm not like that.''

''Too honorable, huh?''

Clarissa looked over at Conor.

''Maybe just foolish,'' she said. ''I've done some very foolish things in my time. Could you track down how the money ended up in the account and send it back where it came from?''

''Sure. It looks like it was in two wire transfers. One last week for two million and one transfer of another million dollars just an hour ago. Let me see if I can pull this up on my computer screen.''

Clarissa held the phone. Out of the corner of her eye, she suddenly noticed Conor's big wide cocky grin.

Several strands of thought came together.

The initial meeting at the University Club—his presence there had never been fully explained.

The laughter of Latin's headmaster at all her questions when she wanted references for her new babysitter. Maybe the laughter was directed at her, maybe he had known something she hadn't.

The telephone number to the James Corporation— it had, after all, been the last Conor James in the phone book.

And then the way Conor dodged the issue of work, but always seemed to have money.

In fact, if she thought carefully, he had been as likely to take money for baby-sitting for her as he was to ignore her purse.

Maybe she had been too quick to jump to conclusions.

Maybe he had been willing to lie....

A million. Another million. A third million this afternoon.

"Ms. McShaunessy? I've discovered who made the wire transfers. They were all from a James Corporation and they were authorized by Mr. Conor James—there's been no mistake. Do you need any further information?"

"No, no, that won't be necessary," Clarissa said. The telephone slipped from her hand. She didn't need to hear any more.

"Did you find out how quickly we're going to the poorhouse?" Conor asked sweetly.

"You bastard," she hissed.

"What?" he demanded, all innocent-looking.

Clarissa glowered.

"You played me for a fool," she stormed. "You're rich."

"Yeah, I am," he admitted. "Since you're marrying me, you are, too."

"And you don't have a regular job because you're too rich to need one," she said, circling the bed like a predatory cat.

"Not quite. I own my own business. I come and go as I please." He shrugged. "As long as I get the work done, the money comes in. And it comes in, baby, lots and lots of it. You should be happy about that."

"And you don't have a savings account because…"

"Because the stock market has consistently outperformed interest-bearing accounts. You know, I thought you'd be delighted to find out I was rich."

"I'm not."

"Why not? You get to marry a millionaire."

"You lied to me!" she accused, grabbing a tortoiseshell-handled hairbrush from the vanity and throwing it at him. It missed, but the dent it made in the wall gave him an idea that she wasn't joking.

"I never actually lied," Conor soothed. "All I did was let you think what you wanted. You saw a man who wasn't wearing a three-piece suit and didn't have a ball and chain on him from nine on Monday to five on Friday—and you decided that man must be a jerk. You're the one who came to the conclusion that I was a deadbeat."

"You lied. Letting me think something that's not true is the same as lying to me. You played me for a fool."

He eased out of bed, keeping the sheet wrapped around his torso.

"I thought a lot of things, but fool was never one of them. I admit, I thought you were a jerk. I thought you were a jerk until just about two hours ago. And then I decided I wanted you—no, needed you—to be my wife."

He held out a conciliatory arm to her, but she slapped it away.

"You thought my plan was something to be laughed at."

"No, Clarissa, I never laughed. No, never. I remember being poor. Supporting my mom when I was seventeen because my dad walked out on us. Not knowing where our next meal was coming from, grateful for every scrap of work I could get. I know it's tough out there.''

''And you think I was taking the easy way out?''

''Maybe a little. But I wasn't there for the rest of your life. I don't want to pass judgment on how hard it was.''

She flinched and looked away. And then she was drawn back to him, as surely as a magnet. He put his arms around her and she put up little resistance.

''You have such a tough exterior,'' Conor said. ''But it's okay to not be tough sometimes, to let someone you love carry the burden for a while. Just like when we make love. Don't blush so, don't turn away. Hear me out.''

''Conor, no.''

''Listen, baby. When we make love, you let your guard down. You can do that with me all the time. Even when we're not making love. You're not made of iron. You don't have to be. You're a woman, made of flesh.''

''I bet you're also going to tell me again I'm not millionaire material because I don't want to eat caviar and I'm not from this neighborhood.''

''Baby, if you're not millionaire material, neither am I. We're two of a kind. Because I think the finest dining is hamburgers and a cold beer. And we're moving to Bridgeport. I've bought up a block and I'm developing it. We'll have an apartment there. I think we'll agree that my job is as regular as it gets, I can open up a savings account if you're truly determined, and if you really want me to buy a monkey suit, I will. I'll play by your rules, but you've got to play by mine.''

''You're serious about the buttons?''

''Absolutely.''

''And the cotton underwear?''

''Never more serious in my life,'' he said, fingering the soft-as-cashmere cotton of her tank top.

''And are you going to keep giving me a million dollars every time we make love?''

He kissed her earlobe.

''The first time I wired money into your account, I did it just to show you I wasn't a deadbeat. Today I did it as a wedding present. But if I have to keep giving you a million dollars every time we make love, I swear I'll run out of money by the end of the week,'' he complained, kneeling down at her feet and inhaling the strong vanilla scent of her womanhood. ''I'll be very happy but very broke.''

''Well, I suppose a married woman...'' Clarissa took a sharp breath and struggled to maintain her composure. ''A married woman shouldn't take money for making love to her husband.''

''We'd better get dressed before Tommy and Fred get back,'' Conor said, tracing a lazy line along the smooth skin of her back. ''Hey, what are you doing?''

''Looking at my palm. Sabrina has read my palm many times and she's always predicted the same thing, even when I was ten years old. She said I was going to marry a millionaire, and she was right. It's there, on my palm.''

Holding her hand out for his inspection, Conor looked but found no evidence of fortune in the crisscross lines of his lover's palm.

"I'll bet she says 'you'll marry a millionaire' to lots of girls," he said. "Kind of like saying 'you'll live a long life.' You just happen to be the one she got right."

"But she didn't predict millionaires for Hallie or Maggie."

Conor's eyes narrowed.

"Who are they?"

"My girlfriends."

"And they had their fortunes done?"

"Yeah, every year at the Summerfest. Maggie would come from Texas to visit Hallie. They're cousins. Sabrina would read our palms for a quarter."

"What are you talking about?"

Clarissa told him about the summer festival and about Sabrina's fortunes for her two girlfriends. She explained to him how her wish to believe in Sabrina had pushed her into her calculating plan to marry a millionaire—to make her fortune happen.

After all, it was the fortune she had lived with for twenty years.

"So what happened to Maggie and Hallie?"

"They're not married yet," Clarissa said, rolling over and pulling the sheets to her breasts. She wondered if she would ever get used to the brazen way that he regarded her body.

"So maybe Sabrina got it wrong for them. Maybe they're never going to marry. Or they're going to marry dentists or accountants or gym teachers. Or guys from three blocks away instead of next door. Or maybe they're not even thinking about what Sabrina found on their palm.''

''Oh, no—they're both thinking about it. A lot. They're near thirty, too. And a woman really thinks about her future when she turns thirty. They'll create their fortune, finding what fate has in store for them. Just like I did.''

''The male population of the United States should be warned about this,'' Conor grumbled.

''Only the cowboys and a certain bad boy who lives on Hallie's block.''

''So you think Hallie will marry the boy next door? Just because Sabrina said it was so?''

''Sure.''

''What about Maggie? Does she want to marry a cowboy?''

''Not a real one, and that's the funny thing. She has a ranch in Texas and plenty of money, but she wants a millionaire.''

''Are all women this calculating about finding their husbands?''

''Only the happy ones,'' Clarissa said, coming to him with an open, full kiss. ''Only the very happy ones.''

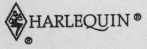

HARLEQUIN®

Don't miss these Harlequin favorites by some of our most distinguished authors!
And now, you can receive a discount by ordering two or more titles!

HT#25645	THREE GROOMS AND A WIFE by JoAnn Ross	$3.25 U.S. $3.75 CAN.	☐
HT#25647	NOT THIS GUY by Glenda Sanders	$3.25 U.S. $3.75 CAN.	☐
HP#11725	THE WRONG KIND OF WIFE by Roberta Leigh	$3.25 U.S. $3.75 CAN.	☐
HP#11755	TIGER EYES by Robyn Donald	$3.25 U.S. $3.75 CAN.	☐
HR#03416	A WIFE IN WAITING by Jessica Steele	$3.25 U.S. $3.75 CAN.	☐
HR#03419	KIT AND THE COWBOY by Rebecca Winters	$3.25 U.S. $3.75 CAN.	☐
HS#70622	KIM & THE COWBOY by Margot Dalton	$3.50 U.S. $3.99 CAN.	☐
HS#70642	MONDAY'S CHILD by Janice Kaiser	$3.75 U.S. $4.25 CAN.	☐
HI#22342	BABY VS. THE BAR by M.J. Rodgers	$3.50 U.S. $3.99 CAN.	☐
HI#22382	SEE ME IN YOUR DREAMS by Patricia Rosemoor	$3.75 U.S. $4.25 CAN.	☐
HAR#16538	KISSED BY THE SEA by Rebecca Flanders	$3.50 U.S. $3.99 CAN.	☐
HAR#16603	MOMMY ON BOARD by Muriel Jensen	$3.50 U.S. $3.99 CAN.	☐
HH#28885	DESERT ROGUE by Erine Yorke	$4.50 U.S. $4.99 CAN.	☐
HH#28911	THE NORMAN'S HEART by Margaret Moore	$4.50 U.S. $4.99 CAN.	☐

(limited quantities available on certain titles)

	AMOUNT	$
DEDUCT:	**10% DISCOUNT FOR 2+ BOOKS**	$
ADD:	**POSTAGE & HANDLING**	$
	($1.00 for one book, 50¢ for each additional)	
	APPLICABLE TAXES*	$
	TOTAL PAYABLE	$
	(check or money order—please do not send cash)	

To order, complete this form and send it, along with a check or money order for the total above, payable to Harlequin Books, to: **In the U.S.:** 3010 Walden Avenue, P.O. Box 9047, Buffalo, NY 14269-9047; **In Canada:** P.O. Box 613, Fort Erie, Ontario, L2A 5X3.

Name:_____

Address: _____ City: _____

State/Prov.:_____ Zip/Postal Code: _____

*New York residents remit applicable sales taxes.
 Canadian residents remit applicable GST and provincial taxes.
Look us up on-line at: http://www.romance.net

HBACK-JM4

And the Winner Is...

You, when you pick up these great titles
from our new promotion at your
favorite retail outlet this February!

Diana Palmer
The Case of the Mesmerizing Boss

Betty Neels
The Convenient Wife

Annette Broadrick
Irresistible

Emma Darcy
A Wedding to Remember

Rachel Lee
Lost Warriors

Marie Ferrarella
Father Goose

Look us up on-line at: http://www.romance.net   ATWI397

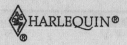 

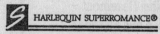 

Harlequin® Historical

If you're a serious fan of historical romance,
then you're in luck!

Harlequin Historicals brings you
stories by bestselling authors, rising new stars
and talented first-timers.

Ruth Langan & Theresa Michaels
Mary McBride & Cheryl St.John
Margaret Moore & Merline Lovelace
Julie Tetel & Nina Beaumont
Susan Amarillas & Ana Seymour
Deborah Simmons & Linda Castle
Cassandra Austin & Emily French
Miranda Jarrett & Suzanne Barclay
DeLoras Scott & Laurie Grant...

You'll never run out of favorites.

Harlequin Historicals...they're too good to miss!